GEORGE'S SECRET KEY TO THE UNIVERSE

www.kidsatrandomhouse.co.uk

For details of Stephen Hawking's
books for adult readers, see:

www.hawking.org.uk

www.rbooks.co.uk

www.georgessecretkey.com

Endpaper image:
This colour-enhanced view of the Eta Carinae nebula covers an area
50 light years across. It was assembled from 48 images obtained by
Hubble's Advanced Camera for Surveys in 2005. The colours represent
different elements: sulphur (red), hydrogen (green) and oxygen (blue).
The nebula is a large cloud of dust and gas, with a mix of hot, young
stars, dying stars and regions of starbirth.

© NASA/ESA/N. SMITH (University of California, Berkeley)/HUBBLE
HERITAGE TEAM (STScI/AURA)/SCIENCE PHOTO LIBRARY

GEORGE'S SECRET KEY TO THE UNIVERSE

Lucy & Stephen
HAWKING

with Christophe Galfard

Illustrated by Garry Parsons

DOUBLEDAY

GEORGE'S SECRET KEY TO THE UNIVERSE
A DOUBLEDAY BOOK 978 0 385 61181 7 (Cased)
978 0 385 61270 8 (Trade paperback)

Published in Great Britain by Doubleday,
an imprint of Random House Children's Books.
A Random House Group Company.

This edition published 2007

1 3 5 7 9 10 8 6 4 2

The Random House Group Limited makes every effort to ensure that the papers used in its books are
made from trees that have been legally sourced from well-managed and credibly certified forests. Our
paper procurement policy can be found at: www.randomhouse.co.uk/paper.htm

Mixed Sources
Product group from well-managed
forests and other controlled sources
www.fsc.org Cert no. TT-COC-2139
© 1996 Forest Stewardship Council
FSC

Set in 13.5pt Stempel Garamond

RANDOM HOUSE CHILDREN'S BOOKS
61–63 Uxbridge Road, London W5 5SA

www.kidsatrandomhouse.co.uk

Addresses for companies within The Random House Group Limited can be found at:
www.randomhouse.co.uk/offices.htm

THE RANDOM HOUSE GROUP Limited Reg. No. 954009

A CIP catalogue record for this book is available from the British Library.

Printed and bound in
Great Britain by Clays Ltd, St Ives plc

For William and George, with love

Chapter One

Pigs don't just vanish, thought George to himself as he stood staring into the depths of the very obviously empty pigsty. He tried closing his eyes and then opening them again, to see if it was all some kind of horrible optical illusion. But when he looked again, the pig was still gone, his vast muddy pink bulk nowhere to be seen. In fact, when George examined the situation for a second time, it had got worse, not better. The side door of the pigsty, he noticed, was hanging open, which meant someone hadn't shut it properly. And that someone was probably him.

'Georgie!' he heard his mother call from the kitchen. 'I'm going to start supper in a minute so you've only got about an hour. Have you done your homework?'

'Yes, Mum,' he called back in a fake cheery voice.

'How's your pig?'

'He's fine! Fine!' said George squeakily. He threw in a few experimental oinks, just to make it sound as though everything was business as usual, here in the small back garden that was full of many, many vegetables and one enormous – but now mysteriously absent – pig. He grunted a few more times for effect – it was very important his mother did not come out into the garden before George had time to think up a plan. Quite how he was going to find the pig, put it back in the sty, close the door and get back in time for supper, he had no idea. But he was working on it, and the last thing he needed was for one of his parents to appear before he had all the answers.

George knew the pig was not exactly popular with his parents. His mother and father had never wanted a pig in the back garden, and his dad in particular tended to grind his teeth quite hard when he remembered who lived beyond the vegetable patch. The pig had been a

present: one cold Christmas Eve a few years back, a cardboard box full of squeaks and snuffles had been delivered to their front door. When George opened it up, he found a very indignant pink piglet inside. George lifted him carefully out of the box and watched with delight as his new friend

skidded around the Christmas tree on his tiny hooflets. There had been a note taped to the box. *Dear All!* it read. *Happy Christmas! This little chap needs a home – can you give him one? Love Grandma xxx.*

George's dad hadn't been delighted by the new addition to his family. Just because he was a vegetarian, it didn't mean he liked animals. Actually, he preferred plants. They were much easier to deal with: they didn't make a mess or leave muddy trotter prints on the kitchen floor or break in and eat all the biscuits left out on the table. But George was thrilled to have his very own pig. The presents he'd received from his mum and dad that year were, as usual, pretty dreadful. The home-knitted purple and orange striped jumper from his mum had sleeves which stretched right down to the floor; he had never wanted a set of panpipes and he had a hard time looking enthusiastic when he unwrapped a build-your-own-wormery kit.

What George really wanted – above all things in the

Universe – was a computer. But he knew his parents were very unlikely to buy him one. They didn't like modern inventions and tried to do without as many standard household items as they could. Wanting to live a purer, simpler life, they washed all their clothes by hand and didn't own a car and lit the house with candles in order to avoid using any electricity.

It was all designed to give George a natural and improving upbringing, free from toxins, additives, radiation and other such evil phenomena. The only problem was that in getting rid of everything that could

possibly harm George, his parents had managed to do away with lots of things that would also be fun for him. George's parents might enjoy dancing around maypoles, going on eco protest marches or grinding flour to make their own bread, but George didn't. He wanted to go to a theme park and ride on the roller coasters or play computer games or take an aeroplane somewhere far far away. Instead, for now, all he had was his pig.

And a very fine pig he was too. George named him Freddy and spent many happy hours dangling over the edge of the pigsty his father had built in the back garden, watching Freddy rootle around in the straw or snuffle in the dirt. As the seasons changed and the years turned, George's piglet got bigger . . . and bigger . . . and bigger . . . until he was so large that in dim lighting he looked like a baby elephant. The bigger Freddy grew, the more he seemed to feel cooped up in his pigsty. Whenever he got the chance, he liked to escape and rampage across the vegetable patch, trampling on the carrot tops, munching the baby cabbages and chewing up George's mum's flowers. Even though she often told George how important it was to love all living creatures, George suspected that on days when Freddy wrecked her garden, she didn't feel much love for his pig. Like George's dad, his mum was a vegetarian, but George was sure he had heard her angrily mutter 'sausages' under her breath when she was clearing up after one of Freddy's more destructive outings.

On this particular day, however, it wasn't the vege-tables that Freddy had destroyed. Instead of charging madly about, the pig had done something much worse. In the fence that separated George's garden from the one next door, George suddenly noticed a suspiciously pig-sized hole. Yesterday it definitely hadn't been there, but then yesterday Freddy had been safely shut in his sty. And now he was nowhere to be seen. It meant only one thing – that Freddy, in his search for adventure, had burst out of the safety of the back garden and gone somewhere he absolutely should not have done.

Next Door was a mysterious place. It had been empty for as long as George could remember. While all the other terraced houses in the row had neatly kept back gardens, windows which twinkled with light in the evenings and doors that slammed as people ran in and out, this house just sat there – sad, quiet and dark. No small children squeaked with joy early in the morning. No mother called out of the back door to bring people in for supper. At the weekends, there was no noise of hammering nor smell of fresh paint because no one ever came to mend the broken window frames or clear the sagging gutters. Years of neglect meant the garden had rioted out of control until it looked like the Amazon jungle had grown up on the other side of the fence.

On George's side, the back plot was neat, orderly and very boring. There were rows of runner beans strictly tied to stakes, lines of floppy lettuces, frothy

dark green carrot tops and well-behaved potato plants.
George couldn't even kick a ball without it landing *splat*
in the middle of a carefully tended raspberry bush and
squashing it.

George's parents had marked out a little area for
George to grow his own vegetables, hoping he would
become interested in gardening and perhaps grow up
to be an organic farmer. But George preferred looking
up at the sky to looking down at the earth. So his little

patch of the planet stayed bare and scratchy, showing nothing but stones, scrubby weeds and bare ground, while he tried to count all the stars in the sky to find out how many there were.

Next Door, however, was completely different. George often stood on top of the pigsty roof and gazed over the fence into the glorious tangled forest beyond. The sweeping bushes made cosy little hidey-holes while

THE NIGHT SKY

During the day there is only one star that can be seen in the sky. It is the star that is the closest to us, the star that has the most effect on our daily lives and for which we have a special name: the Sun.

The Moon and the planets do not shine on their own. They appear bright at night because the Sun lights them up.

In the night sky there are a few objects that can be seen which are not stars – the Moon and the planets, like Venus, Mars, Jupiter or Saturn.

All the other shining dots in the night sky are stars, like our Sun. Some are bigger, some are smaller, but they are all stars. With a naked eye, on a clear night, away from sources of light like cities, we can see hundreds of them.

the trees had curved, gnarled branches, perfect for a boy to climb. Brambles grew in great clumps, their spiky arms bending into strange, wavy loops, crisscrossing each other like train tracks at a station. In summer, twisty bindweed grasped onto every other plant in the garden like a green cobweb; yellow dandelions sprouted everywhere; prickly poisonous giant hogweed loomed like a species from another planet, while little blue forget-me-not flowers winked prettily in the crazy bright green jumble of Next Door's back garden.

But Next Door was also forbidden territory. George's parents had very firmly said 'No' to the idea of George using it as an extra playground. And it hadn't been their normal sort of 'No', which was a wishy-washy, kindly, we're-asking-you-not-to-for-your-own-sake sort of 'No'. This had been a real 'No', the kind you didn't argue with. It was the same 'No' that George had encountered when he tried suggesting that, as everyone else at school had a television set – some kids even had one in their bedrooms! – maybe his parents could think about buying one. On the subject of television, George had to listen to a long explanation from his father about how watching mindless rubbish would pollute his brain. But when it came to Next Door, he didn't even get a lecture from his dad. Just a flat, conversation-ending 'No'.

George, however, always liked to know *why*. Guessing he wasn't going to get any more answers from his dad, he asked his mother instead.

'Oh, George,' she had sighed as she chopped up Brussels sprouts and turnips and threw them into the cake mix. She tended to cook with whatever came to hand rather than with ingredients that would actually combine to make something tasty. 'You ask too many questions.'

'I just want to know *why* I can't go next door,' George persisted. 'And if you tell me, I won't ask any more questions for the whole of the rest of the day. I promise.'

His mum wiped her hands on her flowery apron and took a sip of nettle tea. 'All right, George,' she said. 'I'll tell you a story if you stir the muffins.' Passing over the big brown mixing bowl and the wooden spoon, she settled herself down as George started to beat the stiff yellow dough with the green and white vegetable speckles together.

'When we first moved here,' his mum began, 'when you were very small, an old man lived in that house. We hardly ever saw him but I remember him well. He had the longest beard I've ever seen – it went right down to his knees. No one knew how old he really was but the neighbours said he'd lived there for ever.'

'What happened to him?' asked George, who'd already forgotten that he'd promised not to ask any more questions.

'Nobody knows,' said his mum mysteriously.

'What do you mean?' asked George, who had stopped stirring.

'Just that,' said his mum. 'One day he was there. The next day he wasn't.'

'Perhaps he went on holiday,' said George.

'If he did, he never came back,' said his mum. 'Eventually they searched the house but there was no sign of him. The house has been empty ever since and no one has ever seen him again.'

'Gosh,' said George.

'A little while back,' his mum continued, blowing on her hot tea, 'we heard noises next door – banging sounds in the middle of the night. There were flashing lights and voices as well. Some squatters had broken in and were living there – the police had to throw them out. Just last week we thought we heard the noises again. We don't know who might be in that house. That's why your dad doesn't want you going round there, Georgie.'

As George looked at the big black hole in the fence, he remembered the conversation he'd had with his mum. The story she'd told him hadn't stopped him from wanting to go Next Door – it still looked mysterious and enticing. But wanting to go Next Door when he knew he couldn't was one thing; finding out he actually *had* to was quite another. Suddenly Next Door seemed dark, spooky and very scary.

George felt torn. Part of him just wanted to go home to the flickery candlelight and funny familiar smells of his mother's cooking; to close the back door and be safe and snug inside his own house once more. But that would mean leaving Freddy alone and possibly in danger. He couldn't ask his parents for any help in case they decided that this was the final black mark against Freddy's name and packed him off to be made into bacon rashers. Taking a deep breath, George decided he had to do it. He had to go Next Door.

Closing his eyes, he plunged through the hole in the fence.

When he came out on the other side and opened his eyes, he was right in the middle of the jungle garden. Above his head, the tree cover was so dense he could hardly see the sky. It was getting dark now and the thick forest made it even darker. George could just see where a path had been trampled through the enormous weeds. He followed it, hoping it would lead him to Freddy.

He waded through great banks of brambles, which

grabbed at his clothes and scratched his bare skin. They seemed to reach out in the semi-darkness to scrape their prickly spines along his arms and legs. Muddy old leaves squidged under his feet and nettles attacked him with their sharp, stinging fingers. All the while the wind in the trees above him made a singing, sighing noise as though the leaves were saying, *Be careful, Georgie . . . be careful, Georgie.*

The trail brought George into a sort of clearing, right behind the house itself. So far he had not seen or heard any sign of his naughty pig. But there, on the broken paving stones outside the back door, he saw only too clearly a set of muddy trotter prints. From the marks, George could tell exactly which way Freddy had gone. His pig had marched straight into the abandoned house through the back door, which had been pushed open just wide enough for a fat pig to squeeze through. Worse, from the house where no one had lived for years and years shone a beam of light.

Somebody was home.

Chapter Two

George looked back down the garden, at the path along which he'd come. He knew he should go back and get his parents. Even if he had to admit to his dad that he'd climbed through the fence into Next Door's garden, it would still be better than standing there all alone. He would just peek through the window to see if he could catch a glimpse of Freddy and then he would go and fetch his dad.

He edged closer to the beam of bright light coming from the empty house. It was a golden colour, quite unlike the weak candlelight in his own house or the cold blue neon strips at school. Even though he was so scared his teeth had started to chatter, the light seemed to draw him forward until he was standing right by the window. He peered closer. Through the narrow space between the window frame and the blind he could just see into the house. He could make out a kitchen, littered with mugs and old tea bags.

A sudden movement caught his eye and he squinted down at the kitchen floor, where he saw Freddy, his

pig! He had his snout in a bowl and was slurping away, drinking his fill of some mysteriously bright purple liquid.

George's blood ran cold – it was a terrible trick, he just *knew* it. 'Yikes!' he shouted. 'It's poison.' He rapped sharply on the pane of glass. '*Don't drink it, Freddy!*' he yelled.

But Freddy, who was a greedy pig, ignored his master's voice and carried on happily hoovering up the contents of the bowl. Without stopping to think, George flew through the door and into the kitchen, where he grabbed the bowl from under Freddy's snout and threw its contents down the sink. As the violet-coloured liquid gurgled down the plughole, he heard a voice behind him.

'Who,' it said, in distinct but childish tones, 'are *you*?'

George whirled round. Standing behind him was a girl. She was wearing the most extraordinary costume, made of so many different colours and flimsy layers of fabric that it looked as though she had rolled herself in butterfly wings.

George spluttered. She might look strange, this girl with her long tangled blonde hair and her blue and green feathery headdress, but she definitely wasn't scary. 'Who,' he replied indignantly, 'do you think *you* are?'

'I asked first,' said the girl. 'And anyway, this is *my* house. So I get to know who you are but I don't have to say anything if I don't want to.'

'I'm George.' He stuck out his chin as he always did when he felt cross. 'And that' – he pointed to Freddy – 'is my pig. And you've kidnapped him.'

'I haven't kidnapped your pig,' said the girl hotly. 'How stupid. What would I want a pig for? I'm a ballerina and there aren't any pigs in the ballet.'

'Huh, ballet,' muttered George darkly. His parents had made him take dance classes when he was younger and he'd never forgotten the horror. 'Anyway,' he retorted, 'you're not old enough to be a ballerina. You're just a kid.'

'Actually, I'm in the corps de ballet,' said the girl snootily. 'Which shows how much *you* know.'

'Well, if you're so grown up, why were you trying to poison my pig?' demanded George.

'That's not poison,' said the girl scornfully. 'That's Ribena. It's a juice made from blackcurrants – I thought *everyone* knew that.'

George, whose parents only ever gave him cloudy, pale, home-pressed fruit juices, suddenly felt very silly for not realizing what the purple stuff was.

'Well, this isn't really your house, is it?' he continued, determined to get the better of her somehow. 'It belongs to an old man with a long beard who disappeared years ago.'

'This *is* my house,' said the girl, her blue eyes flashing. 'And I live here except when I'm dancing on stage.'

'Then where are your mum and dad?' demanded George.

'I don't have any parents.' The girl's pink lips stuck out in a pout. 'I'm an orphan. I was found backstage wrapped up in a tutu. I've been adopted by the ballet. That's why I'm such a talented dancer.' She sniffed loudly.

'Annie!' A man's voice rang through the house. The

girl stood very still.

'Annie!' They heard the voice again, coming closer. 'Where are you, Annie?'

'Who's that?' asked George suspiciously.

'That's . . . er . . . that's . . .' She suddenly became very interested in her ballet shoes.

'Annie, there you are!' A tall man with messy dark hair and thick, heavy-framed spectacles, set at a crooked angle on his nose, walked into the kitchen. 'What have you been up to?'

'Oh!' The girl flashed him a brilliant smile. 'I've just been giving the pig a drink of Ribena.'

A look of annoyance crossed the man's face. 'Annie,' he said patiently, 'we've talked about this. There are times to make up stories. And there are times . . .' He trailed off as he caught sight of George standing in the corner and, next to him, a pig with blackcurrant stains around his snout and mouth that made him look as though he were smiling.

'Ah, a pig . . . In the kitchen . . . I see . . .' he said slowly, taking in the scene. 'Sorry, Annie, I thought you were making things up again. Well, hello.' The man crossed the room to shake hands with George. Then he sort of patted the pig rather gingerly between the ears. 'Hello . . . Hi . . .' He seemed unsure what to say next.

'I'm George,' said George helpfully. 'And this is my pig. Freddy.'

'Your pig,' the man echoed. He turned back to Annie, who shrugged and gave him an I-told-you-so look.

'I live next door,' George went on by way of explanation. 'But my pig escaped through a hole in the fence so I had to come and get him.'

'Of course!' The man smiled. 'I was wondering how you got into the kitchen. My name is Eric – I'm Annie's dad.' He pointed to the blonde girl.

'Annie's dad?' said George slyly, smiling at the girl. She stuck her nose up in the air and refused to meet his eye.

'We're your new neighbours,' said Eric, gesturing around the kitchen, with its peeling wallpaper, mouldy old tea bags, dripping taps and torn floor covering. 'It's a bit of a mess. We haven't been here long. That's why we haven't met before.' Eric ruffled his dark hair and frowned. 'Would you like something to drink? I gather Annie's already given your pig something.'

'I'd love some Ribena,' said George quickly.

'None left,' said Annie, shaking her head. George's face fell. It seemed very hard luck that even Freddy the pig should get to have nice drinks when he didn't.

Eric opened a few cupboards in the kitchen but they were all empty. He shrugged apologetically. 'Glass of water?' he offered, pointing to the tap.

George nodded. He wasn't in a hurry to get home for his supper. Usually when he went to play with other kids, he went back to his own mum and dad feeling

depressed by how peculiar they were. But this house seemed so odd that George felt quite cheerful. Finally he had found some people who were even odder than his own family. But just as he was thinking these happy thoughts, Eric went and spoiled it for him.

'It's rather dark,' he said, peering out of the window. 'Do your parents know you're here, George?' He picked up a telephone handset from the kitchen counter. 'Let's give them a call so they don't worry about you.'

'Erm . . .' said George awkwardly.

'What's the number?' asked Eric, looking at him over

the top of his glasses. 'Or are they easier to reach on a mobile?'

'They, er . . .' George could see no way out. 'They don't have any kind of phone,' he said in a rush.

'Why not?' said Annie, her blue eyes very round at the thought of not owning even a mobile.

George squirmed a bit; both Annie and Eric were looking at him curiously so he felt he had to explain. 'They think technology is taking over the world,' he said very quickly. 'And that we should try and live without it. They think that people – because of science and its discoveries – are polluting the planet with modern inventions.'

'Really?' Eric's eyes sparkled behind his heavy glasses. 'How very interesting.' At that moment the phone in his hand burst into tinkling song.

'Can I get it can I get it? Pleasepleaseplease?' said Annie, grabbing the phone from him. 'Mum!' And with a shriek of joy and a flounce of brightly coloured costume, she shot out of the kitchen, phone clasped to her ear. 'Guess what, Mum!' Her shrill voice rang out as she pattered along the hall corridor. 'A strange boy's come round . . .'

George went bright red with embarrassment.

'And he has a pig!' Annie's voice carried perfectly back to the kitchen.

Eric peered at George and gently eased the kitchen door closed with his foot.

'And he's never had Ribena!' Her fluting tones could still be heard through the shut door.

Eric turned on the tap to get George a glass of water.

'And his parents don't even have a phone!' Annie was fainter now but they could still make out each painful word.

Eric flicked on the radio and music started playing. 'So, George,' he said loudly, 'where were we?'

'I don't know,' whispered George, who could barely be heard in the din Eric had created in the kitchen to block out Annie's telephone conversation.

Eric threw him a sympathetic glance. 'Let me show you something fun,' he shouted, producing a plastic ruler from his pocket. He brandished it in front of George's nose. 'Do you know what this is?' he asked at top volume.

'A ruler?' said George. The answer seemed a bit too obvious.

'That's right,' cried Eric, who was now rubbing the ruler against his hair. 'Watch!' He held the ruler near the thin stream of water running from the tap. As he did so, the stream of water bent in the air and flowed at an angle rather than straight down. Eric took the ruler away from the water and it ran down normally again. He gave the ruler to George, who rubbed it in his hair and put it close to the stream of water. The same thing happened.

'Is that magic?' yelled George with sudden excitement,

completely distracted from Annie's rudeness. 'Are you a wizard?'

'Nope,' said Eric, putting the ruler back in his pocket as the water ran down in a long straight line once more. He turned off the tap and switched off the radio. It was quiet now in the kitchen and Annie could no longer be heard in the distance.

'That's science, George,' said Eric, his whole face shining. 'Science. The ruler steals electric charges from your hair when you rub the ruler through it. We can't see the electric charges, but the stream of water can feel them.'

'Gosh, that's amazing,' breathed George.

'It is,' agreed Eric. 'Science is a wonderful and fascinating subject which helps us understand the world around us and all its marvels.'

'Are you a scientist?' asked George. He suddenly felt very confused.

'I am, yes,' replied Eric.

'Then how can that' – George pointed at the tap – 'be science when science is also killing the planet and everything on it? I don't understand.'

'Ah, clever boy,' said Eric with a flourish. 'You've got right to the heart of the matter. I shall answer your question, but to do so, first I need to tell you a bit about science itself. Science is a big word. It means explaining the world around us using our senses, our intelligence and our powers of observation.'

'Are you sure?' asked George doubtfully.

'Very sure,' said Eric. 'There are many different types of natural science and they have many different uses. The one I work with is all about the How and the Why. How did it all begin – the Universe, the Solar System, our planet, life on Earth? What was there before it began? Where did it all come from? And how does it all work? And why? This is physics, George, exciting, brilliant and fascinating physics.'

'But that's really interesting!' exclaimed George. Eric was talking about all the questions he pestered his parents with – the ones they could never answer. He tried asking these big questions at school but the answer he got most often was that he'd find out in his classes the following year. That wasn't really the reply he was after.

'Shall I carry on?' Eric asked him, his eyebrows raised.

George was just about to say 'Oh, yes please,' when Freddy, who had been quiet and docile up till then, seemed to pick up on his excitement. He lumbered to his trotters and, with a surprising spurt of speed, he dashed forward, ears flattened, hooves flying, towards the door.

'*No-o-o-o-o!*' cried Eric, throwing himself after the pig, who had barged through the kitchen door.

'*Sto-o-o-op!*' shouted George, rushing into the next room behind them.

'Oink oink oink oink oink oink!' squealed Freddy, who was obviously enjoying his day out enormously.

Chapter Three

If George had thought the kitchen was untidy, then this next room was in a whole different dimension of messiness. It was filled with piles and piles of books, stacked up so high that some of the wobbly towers reached almost to the ceiling. As Freddy charged right through the middle of the room, notebooks, paperbacks, leather-bound tomes and bits of paper flew up in a tornado around him.

'Catch him!' shouted Eric, who was trying to drive the pig back towards the kitchen.

'I'm trying!' George shouted back as he was batted in the face by a shiny jacketed book.

'Hurry!' said Eric. 'We must get him out of here.'

With a great leap, Annie's dad hurled himself right onto Freddy's back and grabbed his ears. Using them as a sort of steering wheel, he turned the pig – who was still moving at quite some speed – and rode him like a bucking bronco through the door and back into the kitchen.

Left alone, George looked around in wonder. He had never been in a room like this before. Not only was it beautifully, gloriously messy as all the papers flying about in the air came gently down to the ground, but it was also full of exciting objects.

On the wall, a huge blackboard covered in symbols

and squiggles in coloured chalk caught his eye. It also had lots of writing on it but George didn't stop to read it. There were too many other things to look at. In the corner, a grandfather clock ticked slowly, the noise of the swinging pendulum clicking in time with a row of silvery balls suspended on very fine wire which seemed to be in perpetual motion. On a wooden stand was a long brass tube which pointed up towards the window. It looked old and beautiful and George couldn't resist touching the metal, which felt cool and soft at the same time.

Eric walked back into the room, his shirt untucked, his hair standing on end, his glasses at a strange angle

and a huge smile on his face. In his hand he held a book, which he had caught while riding Freddy out of the room.

'George, this is brilliant!' Eric looked thrilled. 'I thought I'd lost it – it's my new book! I couldn't see it anywhere. And now your pig has found it for me! What a result!'

George just stood there, hand on the metal tube, staring at Eric open-mouthed. He'd been expecting to get into trouble for the damage his pig had wreaked. But Eric didn't even seem angry. He wasn't like anyone George had ever met – he never seemed to get cross, no matter what happened in his house. It was all very baffling.

'So I must thank you for all your help today,' continued the peculiar Eric, putting the lost book on top of a cardboard box.

'Help?' echoed George faintly, who couldn't quite believe what he was hearing.

'Yes, help,' said Eric firmly. 'As you seem so interested in science, perhaps I could tell you a bit more about it, by way of a thank you. Where shall we start? What would you like to know?'

George's mind was so full of questions that he found it hard to pick just one. Instead, he pointed at the metal tube. 'What's this?' he asked.

'Good choice, George, good choice,' said Eric happily. 'That's my telescope. It's a very old one – four hundred years ago it belonged to a man called Galileo. He lived in Italy and he loved looking up at the sky at night. At that time, people believed that all the planets in our Solar System went around the Earth – even the Sun, they thought, orbited our planet.'

'But I know that's not true,' said George, putting his eye to the old telescope. 'I know that the Earth goes around the Sun.'

'You do now,' said Eric. 'Science is also about gaining knowledge through experience – you know that fact because Galileo discovered it all those years ago. By looking through his telescope, he realized that the Earth and all the other planets in the Solar System orbit the Sun. Can you see anything?'

'I can see the Moon,' said George, squinting up the telescope, which was angled to look out of the sitting-room window up into the evening sky. 'It looks like it's smiling.'

'Those are scars from a violent past, the impacts of meteorites that crashed on the surface,' said Eric. 'You can't see very far with Galileo's telescope, but if you went to an observatory and looked through a really big telescope, you would be able to see stars billions and billions of miles away – stars so far away that by the time their light reaches our planet, they may actually already be dead.'

'Can a star die? Really?' asked George.

'Oh yes,' said Eric. 'But first I want to show you how

OUR MOON

- **A moon is a natural satellite of a planet.**
- **A satellite is an object that goes around a planet, like the Earth goes around the Sun, and natural means that it is not man-made.**

Average distance from the Earth: 238,854 miles (384,399 kilometres)

Diameter: 2,160 miles (3,476 km), which is 27.3% of Earth's diameter
Surface area: 0.074 x Earth's surface area **Volume:** 0.020 x Earth's volume **Mass:** 0.0123 x Earth's mass **Gravity at the equator:** 16.54% of Earth's gravity at Earth's equator.

The most obvious effect the Moon's gravity has on the Earth is the tides of the oceans. The sea on the side of the Earth facing the Moon is pulled harder towards the Moon because it is nearer. This raises a bulge in the sea on that side. Similarly the sea on the side away from the Moon is pulled towards the Moon less than the Earth because it is further away. This creates another bulge in the sea on the other side of the Earth.

Even though the Sun's gravitational pull is much stronger than the Moon's, it has only about half the Moon's effect on the tides because it is so much further away. When the Moon is roughly in line with the Earth and the Sun, the Moon and the Sun tides add together to produce the large tides (called 'spring tides') twice a month.

The Moon circles around the Earth in 27.3 days.

The way the Moon shines in the night sky is the same every 29.5 days.

There is no atmosphere on the Moon, so the sky there is black, even during the day. And there hasn't been an earthquake or volcanic eruption there since around the time life began on Earth. So all living organisms that have ever been on the Earth have seen exactly the same features on the Moon.

From Earth, we always see the same side of the Moon. The first pictures of the Moon's hidden side were taken by a spacecraft in 1959.

a star is born and then we'll take a look at how it dies. Hang on a minute, George, while I get everything set up – I think you're going to like this.'

LIGHT & STARS

☆ Everything in our Universe takes time to travel, even light.

☆ In space, light always travels at the maximum speed that is possible: 186,000 miles per second (300,000 km per second). This speed is called the speed of light.

☆ It only takes light about 1.3 seconds to travel from Earth to the Moon.

☆ Our Sun is further away from us than our Moon is.

☆ When light leaves the Sun, it takes about 8 minutes and 30 seconds to reach us on Earth.

★ The other stars in the sky are much, much further away from Earth than the Sun. The closest one after the Sun is called Proxima Centauri and it takes 4.22 years for light from it to reach Earth.

★ All other stars are even further away. The light of almost all the stars we can see in the night sky has been travelling for hundreds, thousands or even tens of thousands of years before reaching our eyes. Even though we see them, some of these stars may not exist any more, but we do not know it yet because the light of their explosion when they die has yet to reach us.

★ Distances in space can be measured in terms of light-years, which is the distance light travels in one year. A light-year is almost 6,000 billion miles (around 9,500 billion km).

© ANGLO-AUSTRALIAN OBSERVATORY/DSS/DAVID MALIN IMAGES

Proxima Centauri, the closest star to the Earth after our Sun.

Chapter Four

Eric walked towards the door and stuck his head out through it into the hallway. 'Ann-ie!' he shouted up the stairs.

'Ye-e-e-es,' her distant voice tinkled down to them.

'Do you want to come and see *The Birth and Death of a Star*?' called Eric.

'Seen it already,' she sang back. 'Loads of times.' They heard her feet pattering down the stairs, and a second later she stuck her head round the door. 'Can I have some crisps?'

'If we've got any,' replied Eric. 'And if we do, you're to bring them into my library and share them with George. OK?'

Annie smiled sweetly and disappeared into the

kitchen. They heard the noise of cupboard doors being flung open.

'You mustn't mind Annie,' said Eric gently, without looking at George. 'She doesn't mean any harm. She's just . . .' He trailed off and went over to the far corner of the room, where he started fiddling around with a computer George hadn't noticed before. He'd been too fascinated by the other objects to look at the flat silver screen with its keyboard attached. It was strange that George hadn't spotted the computer straight away – he really wished he could persuade his mum and dad to buy him one. He was saving up his pocket money for a computer but at the current rate (50p a week), he calculated it was going to take him about eight years to afford even a really rubbish second-hand one. So instead, he had to use the clunky, slow old machines at school that crashed every five minutes and had sticky fingerprints all over the screen.

Eric's computer was small and glossy. It looked powerful and neat – the sort of computer you might find on a spaceship. Eric hit a couple of buttons on the keyboard and the computer

made a sort of humming noise while bright flashes of colour shot across the screen. He patted the computer happily.

'You have forgotten something,' said a strange mechanical voice. George jumped out of his skin.

'Have I?' Eric looked confused for a moment.

'Yes,' said the voice. 'You have not introduced me.'

'I'm so sorry!' exclaimed Eric. 'George, this is Cosmos, my computer.'

George gulped. He had no idea what to say.

'You have to say hello to Cosmos,' said Eric in a side whisper to George. 'Otherwise he'll get offended.'

'Hello, Cosmos,' said George nervously. He'd never spoken to a computer before and he didn't quite know where to look.

'Hello, George,' replied Cosmos. 'Eric, you have forgotten something else.'

'What now?' said Eric.

'You have not told George I am the most powerful computer in the world.'

Eric threw his eyes up to heaven. 'George,' he said patiently, 'Cosmos is the most powerful computer in the world.'

'That is correct,' agreed Cosmos. 'I am. In the future, there will be computers more powerful than me. But there are none in the past or present.'

'Sorry about this,' Eric whispered to George. 'Computers can be a bit touchy sometimes.'

'I am cleverer than Eric too,' boasted Cosmos.

'Says who?' said Eric crossly, glaring at the screen.

'Says me,' said Cosmos. 'I can compute billions of numbers in a nanosecond. In less time than it takes you to say "Cosmos is great", I can compute the life of planets, of comets, of stars and of galaxies. Before you can say "Cosmos is the most impressive computer that I have ever seen, he is truly incredible", I can—'

'All right, all right,' said Eric. 'Cosmos, you are the most impressive computer we have ever seen. Now, can we get on? I want to show George how a star is born.'

'No,' said Cosmos.

'*No?*' said Eric. 'What do you mean, *No,* you ridiculous machine?'

'I don't want to,' said Cosmos snootily. 'And I am not ridiculous. I am the most powerful computer that has ever been—'

'Oh but *ple-e-ease,*' pleaded George, interrupting him. 'Please, Cosmos, I really want to see how a star is born. *Please* won't you show me?'

Cosmos was silent.

'Oh go on, Cosmos,' said Eric. 'Let's show George some of the wonders of the Universe.'

'Maybe,' replied Cosmos sulkily.

'George doesn't have a very high opinion of science,' Eric went on. 'So this is our chance, Cosmos, to show him the other side of science.'

'He must take the Oath,' said Cosmos.

'Good point – clever Cosmos,' said Eric, leaping over to the blackboard.

George turned and studied the writing on it more closely – it looked like a poem.

'George,' said Eric, 'do you want to learn about the greatest subject in the whole Universe?'

'Oh yes!' exclaimed George.

'Are you prepared to take a special oath to do so? To promise that you will use your knowledge only for good and not for evil?' Eric was staring at George intently from behind his big glasses. His voice had changed – he now sounded extremely serious. 'This is very important, George. Science can be a force for good but, as you pointed out to me earlier, it can also do great harm.'

George stood up straighter and looked Eric in the eye. 'I am,' he confirmed.

'Then,' said Eric, 'look at the words on the blackboard. It is the Oath of the Scientist. If you agree with it, then read the Oath out loud.'

George read what was written on the blackboard and thought about it for a moment. The words of the Oath didn't frighten him. Instead they made him feel tingly with excitement, right down to his toes. He read the Oath out loud, as Eric had instructed.

'*I swear to use my scientific knowledge for the good of Humanity. I promise never to harm any person in my search for enlightenment . . .*'

The sitting-room door opened and Annie sidled in, clutching a huge multipack bag of crisps.

'Carry on,' said Eric encouragingly. 'You're doing very well.'

George read out the next bit.

'*I shall be courageous and careful in my quest for greater knowledge about the mysteries that surround us.*

I shall not use scientific knowledge for my own personal gain or give it to those who seek to destroy the wonderful planet on which we live.

'*If I break this Oath, may the beauty and wonder of the Universe for ever remain hidden from me.*'

Eric clapped. Annie burst an empty crisp packet. Cosmos flashed a rainbow of bright colours across his screen.

'Well done, George,' said Eric. 'You are now the second youngest member of the Order of Scientific Enquiry for the Good of Humanity.'

'I salute you,' said Cosmos. 'From now on, I will recognize your command.'

'And I'll let you have some crisps!' piped up Annie.

'Annie, shush!' said Eric. 'We're just getting to the good bit. George, you may now use the secret key that unlocks the Universe.'

'Can I?' asked George. 'Where is it?'

'Go over to Cosmos,' said Eric quietly, 'and look at his keyboard. Can you guess which one you need to press? Can you work out which one is the secret key that will unlock the Universe for you? Annie – say nothing!'

George did as he was told. Cosmos might be the world's most powerful computer but his keyboard was just an ordinary, familiar one, with the letters and symbols laid out in the same order as even the crummiest school computer's. George thought hard. Which key would be the one to unlock the Universe for him? He looked again at the keyboard – and suddenly he knew.

'It's this one, isn't it?' he said to Eric, his finger hovering.

Eric nodded. 'Press it, George. To begin.'

George's finger came down on the key marked ENTER.

Suddenly the lights in the room started to fade . . .

'Welcome,' said Cosmos, playing a little computerized fanfare, 'to the Universe.'

Chapter Five

The room was getting darker and darker. 'Come and sit here, George,' called Annie, who had already settled herself on the big comfy sofa. George sat down next to her, and after a few seconds he saw a tiny beam of very bright white light. It came directly from Cosmos's screen. The beam shot out into the middle of the room, where it wavered for a second before it began to sketch a shape in the air. It moved from left to right in a straight line before dropping down towards the floor. Leaving a shining path of light behind it, it turned another corner to make three sides of a rectangle. One more right angle and the beam of light came back to its starting point. For a second, it looked like a flat shape hanging in the air, but suddenly it turned into something real and very familiar.

'But that looks like a—' said George, who could suddenly see what it was.

'A window,' said Eric proudly. 'Cosmos has made us a window on the Universe. Watch closely.'

The beam of light disappeared, leaving the window it had drawn in the middle of Eric's sitting room, hanging

in mid-air. Although the outline was still shining with bright light, it now looked exactly like a real window. It had a big sheet of glass in the pane and a metal frame. Beyond it, there was a view. And that view was not of Eric's house, or of any house, road or town, or anywhere else that George had ever seen before.

Instead, through the window George could see an incredible, vast darkness, peppered with what looked like tiny bright stars. He started to try and count them.

'George,' said Cosmos in his mechanical voice, 'there are billions and billions of stars in the Universe. Unless you are as clever as me, you will not be able to count them all.'

'Cosmos, why are there so many?' asked George in wonder.

'New stars are created all the time,' answered the great computer. 'They are born in giant clouds of dust and gas. I am going to show you how it happens.'

'How long does it take for a star to be born?' George asked.

'Tens of millions of years,' replied Cosmos. 'I hope you are not in a hurry.'

'Tut-tut,' said Eric, sitting cross-legged on the floor beside the sofa, his long thin limbs bent at sharp angles. He looked like a friendly giant spider. 'Don't worry, George, I've speeded it up quite a lot. You'll still get home for dinner. Annie, pass the crisps around. I don't know about you, George, but the Universe always makes me very hungry.'

'Oh dear,' said Annie, sounding embarrassed. There was a rustling noise as she rootled around inside the big bag. 'I'd better get some more.' She leaped off the sofa and dashed back to the kitchen.

As Annie left the room, George noticed something about the view through the window onto outer space: not all of it was covered with little stars. In the bottom corner of the window he saw a patch of total darkness, a place where not a single star shone.

'What's happening there?' He pointed.

'Let's have a look, shall we?' said Eric. He pressed a button on a remote control and the view through the window seemed to zoom towards the dark patch. As they got closer, George realized that an enormous cloud was hovering in that spot. The window kept moving forward until they were right inside the cloud itself, and George could see it was made of gas and dust, just as Cosmos had said.

'What is it?' he asked. 'And where is it?'

'It's a huge cloud in outer space, much bigger than the ones in the sky,' replied Eric, 'made up of tiny, tiny particles which are all floating around inside it. There are so many of these particles that the cloud is enormous – it's so big that you could put millions and millions of Earths inside it. From this cloud, many stars will be born.'

Inside the cloud, George could see the particles

PARTICLES

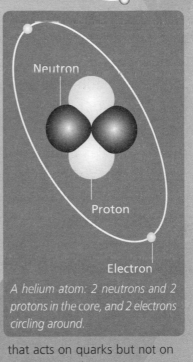

○○○ Elementary particles are the smallest possible things that cannot be divided up into smaller particles. Examples include the electron, which carries electricity, and the photon, which carries light.

○○○ An atom is not an elementary particle because it is made of electrons going around a nucleus in the centre, like the planets go around the Sun. The nucleus is made of protons and neutrons packed tightly together.

○○○ Protons and neutrons were previously thought to be elementary particles but we now know they are made of smaller particles called quarks, held together by gluons, which are the particles of a strong force

Neutron

Proton

Electron

A helium atom: 2 neutrons and 2 protons in the core, and 2 electrons circling around.

that acts on quarks but not on electrons or photons.

moving around, some joining together to form huge lumps of matter. These great lumps spun round and round, gathering even more particles all the time. But as the particles joined together, the spinning lumps weren't getting bigger – instead, they seemed to be getting smaller, as though something was squeezing them. It looked like someone was making gigantic dough balls in outer space. One of these giant balls was quite close to the window now, and George could see it spinning round, getting smaller and smaller all the time. As it shrank, it became hotter and hotter – so hot that George could feel the heat from where he sat on the sofa. And then it started to glow with a dim but frightening light.

'Why is it glowing?' asked George.

'The more it shrinks,' said Eric, 'the hotter it gets. The hotter it gets, the brighter it shines. Very soon it's going to get *too* hot.' He grabbed a couple of pairs of strange sunglasses from a pile of junk on the floor.

'Wear these,' he told George, putting on a pair himself. 'It will soon be too bright for you to look at without glasses.'

Just as George put on the very dark glasses, the ball exploded from the inside, throwing off its outer layers of burning hot gas in all directions. After the explosion, the ball was shining like the Sun.

'Wow!' said George. 'Is that the Sun?'

'It could be,' Eric replied. 'That's how stars are born and the Sun is a star. When a huge

amount of gas and dust combines and shrinks to become dense and hot, as you've just seen, the particles in the middle of the ball are so pressed together they start to fuse or join up, releasing an enormous amount of energy. This is called a *nuclear fusion reaction*. It is so powerful that when it starts, it throws off the outer layers of the ball, and the rest is transformed into a star. That's what you just saw.'

The star was now shining steadily in the distance. It was a beautiful sight. Without the special sunglasses they wouldn't have been able to see much as the star was so bright.

George gazed at it, amazed by its power. Every now and then he could see huge jets of brightly shining gases

MATTER

- Matter is made of atoms of various types. The type of atom or element, as it is called, is determined by the number of protons in the nucleus. This can be up to 118, with mostly an equal or greater number of neutrons.

- The simplest atom is hydrogen, whose nucleus contains just one proton and no neutron.

- The largest naturally occurring atom, uranium, has a nucleus that contains 92 protons and 146 neutrons.

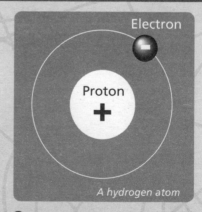

A hydrogen atom

- Scientists think that 90% of the total number of all atoms in the Universe are hydrogen atoms.

sent hundreds of thousands of miles from the surface at extraordinary speeds.

'And the star will keep on shining like this for ever?' he asked.

'Nothing is for ever, George,' said Eric. 'If stars shone for ever, we wouldn't be here. Inside their bellies, stars transform small particles into larger ones. That is what a nuclear fusion reaction does: it fuses small particles together, and builds big atoms out of small ones. The energy released by this fusion is enormous and that's what makes stars shine. Almost all the elements that you and I are made of were built inside stars that existed long before the Earth. So you could say that we are all the children of stars! When they exploded, a long time

- The remaining 10% are all the 117 other atoms, in various proportions. Some are extremely rare.
- When atoms join together in chains, the resulting object is called a molecule. There are countless molecules, of various sizes, and we build new ones all the time in laboratories.
- Before stars are born, only the simplest molecules can be found in space. The most common is the hydrogen molecule, which is inside the huge clouds of gas in outer space where stars are born. It consists of two hydrogen atoms joined together.

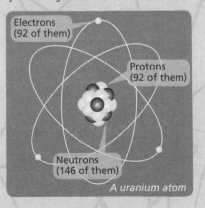

Electrons (92 of them)

Protons (92 of them)

Neutrons (146 of them)

A uranium atom

ago, these stars sent into outer space all these large atoms they created. The same will happen to the star you are looking at now, behind the window. It will explode at the end of its life, when there are no more small particles available to fuse into bigger ones. The explosion will send into outer space all the large atoms the star created in its belly.'

On the other side of the window, the star was looking angry. Its bright yellow colour was turning reddish as it grew and grew, until it was so big that it was almost impossible to see anything else through the window. It seemed to George that the star might explode at any moment. Eric pressed his remote control again and the window immediately moved away from the star, which carried on getting redder and bigger all the time.

'Isn't it amazing!' exclaimed Eric. 'At first the ball shrinks and gives birth to a star, and then the star gets bigger and bigger! And now it is about to explode! Whatever you do, don't take your glasses off.'

George watched the star in fascination. Suddenly, long after it had reached a size no one could have imagined, the most powerful explosion George had ever seen happened just in front of him. The whole star blew up, sending into outer space enormous quantities of light and red-hot gas, including all the new atoms it had created. After the explosion, George saw that all that was left of the star was a beautiful new cloud, full of extraordinary colours and new materials.

'Ooooh-ahhhh!' he said. It was like watching the most incredible firework display.

'You see,' said Eric, 'with time, the colourful cloud you now see will mix with other clouds, ones from far distant stars that have also exploded. As they cool down, all the gases from these clouds will mix together into an even bigger cloud where stars will be born again. Near where these new stars appear, the leftover elements will gather together to become objects of various sizes but not ones big enough to become stars themselves. Some of these objects will become balls and with time, these balls will turn into planets. In real life, it takes a very long time for all this to happen – tens of millions of years!'

'Wow!' George was fascinated.

'But we haven't got that much time to wait, and you need to get home for your supper,' said Eric, going over to Cosmos and pressing a few more keys. 'So let me speed it up a bit. Here we go!'

In the blink of an eye, the tens of millions of years Eric was talking about had passed. The gas from the explosion of dozens of stars had gathered into an immense cloud. Within this cloud, new stars were appearing everywhere, until one formed just in front of the window. That star's brightness made all the other stars very difficult to spot. Some distance away from this new star, the gas left over from the cloud was becoming very cold and had started to gather into small icy rocks. George saw that one of these rocks was heading straight for the window. He opened his mouth to warn Eric, but the rock was travelling far too quickly. Before George could say anything, it smashed into the glass with a shattering, splintering roar, seeming to shake the whole house.

George jumped in fright and fell off the sofa. 'What was *that*?' he shouted to Eric.

'Oops!' said Eric, who was typing away on Cosmos. 'Sorry about that. I wasn't expecting to take a direct hit.'

'You should be more careful,' said Cosmos crossly. 'This isn't the first time we've had an accident.'

'What was it?' asked George, who found he was clutching a small teddy bear that Annie must have left on the sofa. He was feeling rather dizzy.

'We were hit by a tiny comet,' admitted Eric, who

was looking a little sheepish. 'Sorry, everyone. I didn't mean that to happen.'

'A tiny what?' asked George, feeling the room spin around him.

Eric typed a few more commands into Cosmos. 'I think that's enough for today,' he said. 'Are you all right, George?' He took off his glasses and peered into George's face. 'You look a little green.' He sounded worried. 'Oh dear, I thought this was going to be fun. Annie!' he called into the kitchen. 'Can you bring George a glass of water? Oh dear, oh dear.'

Annie came in, walking on tip toes. She was carefully holding a very full teacup of water, some of which was sloshing over the side. Freddy the pig was glued to her side, casting adoring glances up at her with his piggy eyes. She held the cup out to George.

'Don't worry,' she said kindly. 'I felt really sick too, my first time. Dad' – it was a command – 'it's time to let George go home now. He's had enough of the Universe.'

'Yes, yes, I think you're right,' said Eric, still looking concerned.

'But it was so interesting!' protested George. 'Can't I see some more?'

'No, really, I think that's enough,' said Eric hurriedly, putting on a coat. 'I'm going to walk you back to your house now. Cosmos, you're in charge of Annie for a couple of minutes. Come on, George, bring your pig.'

'Can I come back?' said George eagerly.

Eric stopped fussing around with coats and keys and outdoor shoes and smiled. 'I should think so,' he said.

'But you must promise not to tell anyone about Cosmos,' Annie added.

'Is it a secret?' asked George, agog.

'Yes,' said Annie. 'It's a huge great big ginormous amazing secret which is a trillion gazillion times bigger than any secret you've ever heard before.'

'Now, Annie,' said Eric sternly, 'I've told you that gazillion is not a real number. Say goodbye to George and his pig.'

Annie waved and gave George a smile.

'Goodbye, George,' said Cosmos's voice. 'Thank you for making use of my exceedingly powerful capacities.'

'Thank you, Cosmos,' said George politely.

With that, Eric ushered him and Freddy into the hallway and out of the front door and back to their real lives on planet Earth.

Chapter Six

The next day at school, George couldn't stop thinking about the wonders he had seen at Eric's house. Enormous clouds and outer space and flying rocks! Cosmos, the world's most powerful computer! And they all lived next door to him, George, the boy whose parents wouldn't even let him have an ordinary computer in the house. The excitement was almost too much to bear, especially now that George was sitting once more at his very boring desk in the classroom.

He doodled on the schoolbook in front of him with his coloured pencils, trying to sketch Eric's amazing computer – the one that could make a window from thin air, and through that window show you the whole of the birth and death of a star.

But even though George could see it perfectly in his mind, his hand found it difficult to draw a picture that looked anything like what he had seen. It was very annoying. He had to keep crossing bits out and drawing them again, until the whole page looked like one giant squiggle.

'*Ow!*' he exclaimed suddenly as a missile made of a screwed-up ball of paper hit him on the back of the head.

'Ah, George,' said Dr Reeper, his teacher. 'So you are with us this afternoon after all. How nice.'

George looked up with a start. Dr Reeper was standing right over him, staring down through his rather smeared glasses. There was a large blue ink blot on his jacket, which reminded George of the shape of an exploding star.

'Do you have anything to say to the class?' said Dr Reeper, peering down at George's notebook, which

As the Earth's Moon rises just before dawn, Earthshine (sunlight reflected back from the Earth) gently lights up the nightside of the Moon.

© JASON WARE/SCIENCE PHOTO LIBRARY

Although the Moon is usually thought of as grey, it actually has colour. This image has been enhanced to reveal the subtle hues produced by the different geological features of the Moon.

This far side of the Moon can never be seen from Earth. This picture was taken by the *Apollo 16* spacecraft in 1972.

© J-C CUILLANDRE/CANADA-FRANCE-HAWAII TELESCOPE/SCIENCE PHOTO LIBRARY

Because of its distinctive shape, the dark nebula at the centre of this image is called the Horsehead Nebula. It is silhouetted against an emission nebula (called IC 434), which is bright because the hydrogen gas inside it is being lit up by hot stars. It takes light 1,500 years to reach the Earth from there.

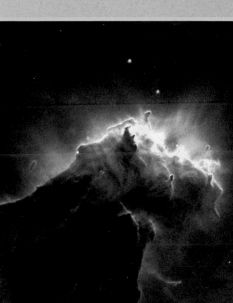

These pillar-shaped cosmic clouds are made of hydrogen and dust. They contain undeveloped stars and are called the Pillars of Creation.

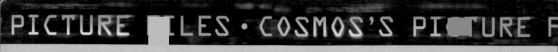

The centre of the Milky Way. This cannot be seen with our eyes because there is cosmic dust in front of it. But this picture was taken in infrared light, which allows us to see hundreds of thousands of hidden stars. Within the white dot at the centre is a supermassive black hole.

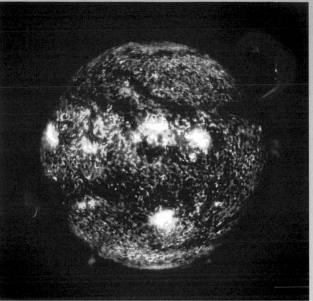

© NASA/SCIENCE PHOTO LIBRARY

An ultraviolet-light picture of the Sun. In the top right of the picture, a hot cloud of plasma (gas) is erupting. This kind of eruption is called a 'solar prominence'.

© ANGLO-AUSTRALIAN OBSERVATORY/DSS/DAVID MALIN IMAGES

Proxima Centauri (the red dot at the centre) is the closest star to the Sun. Light takes 4.22 years to travel from there to the Earth. It takes 8.31 minutes for light to travel from the Sun to the Earth.

George hastily tried to cover. 'Other than "Ow!", the only word I've heard you say today?'

'No, not really,' said George in a strangled, high-pitched voice.

'You wouldn't like to say: "Dear Doctor Reeper, here is the homework I spent all weekend slaving over"?'

'Um, well . . .' said George, embarrassed.

'Or: "Doctor Reeper, I've listened carefully to every word you've ever said in class, written them all down, added my own comments and here is my project, with which you will be extremely pleased"?'

'Er . . .' muttered George, wondering how to get out of this one.

'Of course you wouldn't,' said Dr Reeper heavily. 'After all, I'm just the teacher and I stand here all day saying things for my own amusement and fun, with no hope that anyone will ever gain anything of value from my attempts to educate them.'

'I *do* listen,' protested George, who was now feeling guilty.

'Don't try and flatter me,' said Dr Reeper rather wildly. 'It won't work.' He whipped round sharply. 'And give me that!' He shot across the classroom so fast he was almost a blur of speed and snatched a mobile phone from a boy sitting at the back.

Dr Reeper might wear tweed jackets and speak like a man from a century ago, but his pupils were so scared of him they never played him up in the way they did with teachers who were foolish enough to try and befriend them. He was a new teacher and he hadn't been at the school long, but even on his first day he had quelled a whole room into silence just by staring at them. There was nothing modern or touchy-feely or cosy about Dr Reeper, with the result that his classrooms were always orderly, his homework came in on time and even the slouchy rebel boys sat up straight and fell quiet when he walked into the room.

The kids called him 'Greeper', a nickname that came from the sign on his study door, which read DR G REEPER. Or 'Greeper the Creeper' because of his mysterious habit of appearing without warning in far-flung corners of the school. There would be a gentle *swoosh* of thick-soled shoes and a faint smell of old tobacco, and before anyone knew it, Greeper would be bearing down on whatever secret mischief was brewing, rubbing his scarred hands with delight. No one knew how he had managed to cover both hands in red, scaly, painful-looking burn marks. And no one would ever dare ask.

'Perhaps, George,' said Greeper, pocketing the mobile phone he had just confiscated, 'you would care to enlighten the class as to what the artwork you have been working on this morning represents?'

'It's, well, it's . . .' whispered George, feeling his ears become hot and pink.

'Speak up, boy, speak up!' ordered Greeper. 'We're all agog to know quite what *this*' – he held up George's

drawing of Cosmos so the whole class could see – 'is meant to be! Aren't we, class?'

The other children sniggered, each one of them delighted that Greeper was picking on someone who wasn't them.

At that moment George really hated Greeper. He hated him so much he quite forgot his fear of shame or humiliation in front of the other pupils. Unfortunately he also forgot his promise to Eric.

'It's a very special computer, actually,' he said in a loud voice, 'which can show you what's happening in the Universe. It belongs to my friend Eric.' He fixed Greeper with a very blue stare, his eyes determined under his tufts of dark red hair. 'There are amazing things in outer space, just flying around all the time, like planets and stars and gold and stuff.' George was making the last bit up – Eric hadn't said anything about gold in outer space.

For the first time since George had been in Greeper's class, his teacher seemed lost for words. He just stood there, holding George's book in his hands, his jaw falling open as he looked at George in wonder. 'So it does work, after all,' he half whispered to George. 'And you've seen it. That's amazing . . .' A moment later it seemed as though Greeper were waking from a dream. He snapped George's book shut, handed it back to him and walked to the front of the class.

'Now,' said Greeper loudly, 'given today's behaviour, I'm going to set you all one hundred lines. I want you to write neatly and clearly in your books: *I will not send text messages in Dr Reeper's class because I am too busy listening to all the interesting things he has to say.* One hundred times, please, and anyone who hasn't finished by the time the bell goes can stay behind. Very good, get on with it.'

There was an angry muttering from the classroom. George's classmates had been looking forward to seeing him being taken to pieces by the teacher, and instead, they'd all been punished for something quite different and George had mostly been let off the hook.

'But, sir, that's not fair,' whined a boy at the back.

'Neither is life,' said Greeper happily. 'As that is one of the most useful lessons I could possibly teach you, I feel proud that you've understood it already. Carry on, class.' With that, he sat down at his desk, got out a book that was full of complicated equations and starting flicking through the pages, nodding to himself wisely as he did so.

George felt a ruler being jabbed into his back.

'This is all your fault,' hissed Ringo, the class bully, who was sitting behind him.

'*Silence!*' thundered Greeper, without even looking up from his book. 'Anyone who speaks will do *two* hundred lines instead.'

His hand whizzing across the page, George finished

the one hundred lines in his neat writing just as the bell rang for the end of class. Carefully he tore out the page with the picture of Cosmos on it and folded it up, tucking it into a back trouser pocket before dropping his book on Greeper's desk. But George hadn't taken even two steps down the corridor before Greeper caught up with him and barred his way.

'George,' said Greeper very seriously, 'this computer

is real, isn't it? You've seen it, haven't you?' The look in his eyes was frightening.

'I was just, er, making it up,' said George quickly, trying to wriggle away. He wished he hadn't said anything at all to Greeper.

'Where is it, George?' asked his teacher, speaking slowly and quietly. 'It's very important that you tell me where this amazing computer lives.'

'There *is* no computer,' said George, managing to duck under Greeper's arm. 'It doesn't exist – I just imagined it, that's all.'

Greeper drew back and looked at George thoughtfully. 'Be careful, George,' he said in a scarily quiet voice. 'Be very careful.' With that, he walked away.

Chapter Seven

The way home from school was long and hot; the unexpected heat of the early autumn sun was beating down on the tarmac, turning it soft and squashy under George's feet. He trudged along the pavement while big cars whizzed past him, leaving smelly fumes behind them as they went. In the back of some of these enormous shiny monsters sat the smug kids from school, watching DVDs on the back seat as their parents drove them home. Some of them pulled faces at George as they drove past, jeering at him for having to walk. Others waved happily, as though he would somehow be pleased to see them as they shot off into the distance in their vast gas-guzzlers. No one ever stopped and offered him a lift.

But today he didn't mind. He had plenty to think about on his walk home and he felt glad to be alone. His mind was full of clouds in space, huge explosions and the millions of years it took to make a star. These thoughts took him far, far across the Universe – so far, in fact, that he completely forgot an important fact about his life on planet Earth.

'Oi!' He heard a shout behind him and it snapped him back to the here and now. He hoped it was just someone shouting in the street, a random noise that had nothing to do with him. He hurried along a little faster, clutching his school bag snugly to his chest.

'Oi!' He heard it again, this time a little closer. Resisting the urge to look back, he speeded up his pace. On one side of him was the busy main road, on the other the city park, which offered nowhere to hide. The trees were too thin and straggly to stand behind, and going anywhere near the bushes was a bad idea. The last thing he wanted was to get dragged into them by the boys he feared were behind him. He kept going, getting faster every minute, his heartbeat thumping in his chest like a bongo drum.

'Georgie boy!' He heard the yell and his blood curdled. All his worst fears were confirmed. Usually,

when the end-of-school bell went, George shot out of the gates and was well on his way home while the larger, slower boys were still flicking rubber bands at each other in the cloakroom. He'd heard the awful stories of what Ringo and his followers did to the kids they caught on the street. Eyebrows shaved off, hung upside down, covered in mud, left up a tree wearing only pants, painted in indelible ink or abandoned to take the blame for broken windows – all were whispered tales at school of Ringo's reign of terror.

But on that sunny, drowsy autumn afternoon, George had made a terrible mistake. He was walking home too slowly just when he'd given Ringo and his friends a reason to come looking for him. Angry with him for landing them with extra work in Greeper's class, they were now clearly on his tail and ready to take revenge.

George looked around. Ahead of him he saw a group of mothers pushing prams towards a crossing, where a lollipop lady stopped the traffic to let people across. Scurrying forward, he joined the mums and babies, managing to insert himself in their midst so that he was surrounded by pushchairs. Ambling across the road while the lollipop lady held up her bright yellow sign, George tried to look as though he belonged to one of the mother-and-baby groups. But he knew he wasn't fooling anyone. As he passed the lollipop lady, she winked at him and said under her breath, 'Don't worry, ducks, I'll hold 'em back for you for a minute. But you run along home now. Don't let those nasty boys catch you.'

When George reached the other side of the road, to his surprise the lollipop lady leaned her sign against a tree and stood there, glaring back at Ringo and his mates. The roar of the traffic started up again, and as George sped away he heard another menacing shout.

'Hey! We gotta get across – we need to get home and do our . . . schoolwork . . . If you don't let us cross, I'll tell my mother and she'll come and sort you out . . . she'll give you lollipop, she will . . .'

'You watch yourself, Richard Bright,' grumbled the lollipop lady, walking slowly out into the road with her circular sign.

George turned off the main road, but the sound of heavy thudding feet behind told him they knew which way he'd gone. He was hurrying down a long tree-lined alley which ran behind the gardens of some very big houses; for once it was empty of adults who might have saved him.

George tried a few of the doors in the fences but they were all firmly locked. He looked around in a panic and then had a flash of inspiration. Grabbing onto the lowest bough of an overhanging apple tree, he hoisted himself up high enough to gain a foothold on the top of the fence and leaped right over it. He landed in a large prickly bush, which scratched him, ripping his school uniform. As he lay groaning silently in the shrubbery, he heard Ringo and his mates pass by on the other side of the fence, making spine-chilling comments about what they'd do to George when they got their hands on him.

George stayed still until he was sure they'd gone. Wriggling free of his school jumper, which was hopelessly tangled in the spiky bush, he struggled out of the clinging branches. His trouser pockets had emptied their contents onto the ground. He scrabbled around, trying to collect up all his important bits and pieces. Then he emerged from the undergrowth onto a long, flat green lawn where a very surprised lady lay in a deckchair, sunbathing. She lifted up her dark glasses and looked at him.

'*Bonjour!*' she said in a nice voice. She pointed towards the house. 'Go zat way – ze gate is not so locked.'

'Oh, *merci*,' said George, remembering his one word of French. 'And, er, sorry,' he added as he rushed past her and ran along a passage by the side of her house. He went through the gate, came out onto the road and set off for home, limping a little because he'd twisted his left foot. The streets were quiet and sleepy as he hobbled along. But the silence didn't last long.

'There 'e is!' A great cry went up. '*Georgie-boy!*' he heard. '*We're coming to get you!*'

George gathered the last of his strength and tried to get his legs to move fast but he felt as though he was wading through quicksand. He wasn't far from home – he could see the end of his road – but Ringo and his gang were gaining on him. He ploughed bravely forward, reaching the corner just as he thought he might collapse on the pavement.

'*We're gonna kill you!*' Ringo shouted from behind him.

Staggering, George tottered down his street. His breathing had gone all funny – the air was going in and out of his lungs in great swooshing gasps. All the scratches and bruises and bumps he'd got running away from Ringo were hurting, his throat was parched and he was exhausted. He couldn't have gone much further but he didn't need to – he was home. He'd reached the green front door without being turned into mincemeat, or something worse, by Ringo and his terrible friends, and now everything was going to be all right. All he had to do was reach into his pocket and find his key to unlock the front door.

But it wasn't there.

He turned out his pockets and found all his treasures – his conker, a foreign coin, a length of string, a blob of Blu Tack, a model red sports car and a ball of fluff. But no key. He must have dropped it in the bushes when he climbed over the fence. He rang the bell, hoping his mum might have come home early. *Ting-a-ling-ling-ling!* He tried again. But there was still no answer.

Seeing him standing there, Ringo realized he'd won. He plastered a hideous smile on his face and started to saunter confidently towards George. Behind him, eager for trouble, came his three weasel-faced, hard-knuckled friends.

George knew there was nowhere left to run. He closed his eyes and stood with his back to his front door, his stomach churning as he prepared to meet his fate. He tried to think of something to say which might make Ringo back off. But he couldn't come up with anything clever and there wasn't much point in telling Ringo he was going to get into trouble. Ringo knew that already and it had never stopped him before. The footsteps stopped and George opened one eye to see what was happening. Ringo and his friends had paused halfway down the path and were having some kind of conference about what to do with George.

'No!' Ringo was saying loudly. 'That's rubbish! Let's squeeze him against the wall until he begs us to let him go!'

But just as Ringo spoke, something happened. Something so peculiar that, afterwards, Ringo and his friends weren't sure if they'd dreamed it. The door of the house next to George's flew open and out of it bounded what looked like a tiny astronaut. Everyone took a step back in astonishment as the small figure in a white spacesuit with a round glass helmet, an antenna attached to the back, jumped into the middle of the road, striking a fierce, karate-style pose.

'Get back,' said the spacesuit in a strange metallic voice, 'or I will put the curse of Alien Life on you. You will turn green and your brains will bubble and leak out of your ears and down your nose. Your bones will turn to rubber and you will grow hundreds of warts all over your body. You will only be able to eat spinach and broccoli and you will never ever be able to watch

television again as it will make your eyes fall out of your head. So there!' The astronaut did a few twirls and kicks which looked somehow familiar to George.

Ringo and his friends had turned a ghostly colour and were stumbling backwards, their mouths hanging open. They were absolutely terrified.

'Get into the house,' said the spacesuit to George.

George slipped into Next Door's house. He wasn't scared of the little astronaut – he'd caught a gleam of bright blonde hair through the glass of the helmet. It looked like Annie had saved him.

Chapter Eight

'P hew!' The figure in the spacesuit followed George into the house, slamming the front door with a backward kick of a hefty space boot. 'It's hot in here,' it added, pulling off the round glass helmet and flipping out a long ponytail. It was Annie, a bit pink in the face from jumping about in the heavy suit. 'Did you see how scared they were?' she said to George, beaming and wiping her forehead on her sleeve. 'Did you?' She strode along the hallway, making clunking noises as she walked. 'Come on.'

'Erm, yes. Thank you,' George managed to say as he trailed behind her into the same room where he'd watched *The Birth and Death of a Star* with Eric. He'd been so excited about coming back to see Cosmos again but now he just felt miserable. He'd accidentally told horrible Dr Reeper

about Cosmos when he'd promised Eric he would keep it a secret. He'd had a long frightening journey back from school being chased by the bullies, and to cap it all, he'd been rescued by a little girl wearing a spacesuit. It was turning out to be a really bad day.

Annie, on the other hand, seemed to be enjoying herself no end. 'What do you think?' she said to George, smoothing down the brilliant-white folds of her all-in-one suit. 'It's new – it just arrived in the post.' On the floor lay a cardboard box covered in stamps, marked SPACE ADVENTURES R US! Next to it was a much smaller pink suit with sequins, badges and ribbons sewn all over it. It was dirty and worn and covered in patches. 'That's my old suit,' Annie explained. 'I had that when I was really young,' she said rather scornfully. 'I thought it was cool to put all that stuff on it, but now I like my spacesuits plain.'

'Why have you got a spacesuit?' asked George. 'Are you going to a fancy dress party?'

'As if!' Annie rolled her eyes. 'Cosmos!' she called.

'Yes, Annie,' said Cosmos the computer fondly.

'You good, beautiful, lovely, wonderful computer!'

'Oh, Annie!' said Cosmos, his screen glowing as if he were blushing.

'George wants to know why I have a spacesuit.'

'Annie has a spacesuit,' replied Cosmos, 'so she can go on journeys around outer space. It is very cold out there, around minus two hundred and seventy degrees

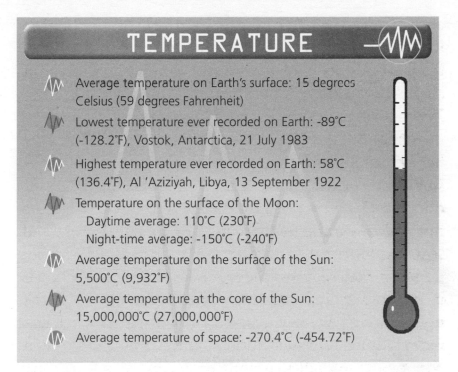

TEMPERATURE

Average temperature on Earth's surface: 15 degrees Celsius (59 degrees Fahrenheit)

Lowest temperature ever recorded on Earth: -89°C (-128.2°F), Vostok, Antarctica, 21 July 1983

Highest temperature ever recorded on Earth: 58°C (136.4°F), Al 'Aziziyah, Libya, 13 September 1922

Temperature on the surface of the Moon:
  Daytime average: 110°C (230°F)
  Night-time average: -150°C (-240°F)

Average temperature on the surface of the Sun: 5,500°C (9,932°F)

Average temperature at the core of the Sun: 15,000,000°C (27,000,000°F)

Average temperature of space: -270.4°C (-454.72°F)

Celsius. She would freeze solid in a fraction of a second if she didn't wear it.'

'Yeah, but—' protested George. But he didn't get far.

'I go on journeys around the Solar System with my dad,' boasted Annie. 'Sometimes my mum comes too but she doesn't really like it in outer space.'

George felt really fed up. He was in no mood for silly games. 'No you don't,' he said crossly. 'You don't go into outer space. You'd have to go up in the space shuttle to do that and they're never going to let you on board because they wouldn't know what was true and what you'd made up.'

Annie's mouth had formed a perfect O.

'You just tell stupid stories about being a ballerina or an astronaut, and your dad and Cosmos pretend to believe you but they don't really,' continued George, who was hot and tired and wanted to have something nice for tea.

Annie blinked rapidly. Her blue eyes were suddenly very shiny and full of tears. 'I'm not making it up,' she said furiously, her round cheeks turning even pinker. 'I'm not, I'm not. It's all true, I don't tell stories. I *am* a ballerina and I *do* go into outer space and I'm going to show you.' She stomped over to Cosmos. 'And,' she went on angrily, 'you're going to come too. And that way you'll believe me.' She rummaged in a packing box and brought out another suit, which she threw at George. 'Put that on,' she commanded.

'Uh-oh,' said Cosmos quietly.

Annie was standing in front of Cosmos, drumming her fingers on the keyboard. 'Where shall I take him?' she asked.

'I don't think this is a good idea,' warned Cosmos. 'What will your dad say?'

'He won't know,' said Annie quickly. 'We'll just go and come straight back. It'll take two minutes. Please, Cosmos!' she pleaded, her eyes now brimming over with tears. 'Everyone thinks I make everything up and I don't! It's true about the Solar System and I want to show George so he doesn't think I tell stories.'

'All right, all right,' said Cosmos hastily. 'Please don't drop salt water on my keyboard, it rusts my insides. But you can just look. I don't want either of you actually to go out there.'

Annie wheeled round to face George. Her face was fierce but the tears were still flowing. 'What do you want to see?' she demanded. 'What's the most interesting thing in the Universe?'

George thought hard. He had no idea what was going on but he certainly hadn't meant to upset Annie so much. He didn't like seeing her cry and now he felt even worse about Eric. Eric had said to him only yesterday that Annie didn't mean any harm and yet George had been quite nasty to her. Perhaps, he thought, it would be better to play along.

'Comets,' he said, remembering the end of *The Birth*

and Death of a Star, and the rock that had smashed into the window. 'I think comets are the most interesting things in the Universe.'

Annie typed the word *Comet* on Cosmos's keyboard.

'Put on your suit, George, quickly!' she ordered. 'It's about to get cold.' With that, she hit the button marked ENTER . . .

Chapter Nine

Once more everything went dark. The little beam of brilliant light shot out from Cosmos's screen into the middle of the room, hovered for a second and then started to draw a shape. Only this time it wasn't making a window out of thin air. It was drawing something different. The beam drew a line up from the floor, then turned left, carried on in a straight line and dropped back down to the floor again.

'Oh, look!' said George, who could see what it was now. 'Cosmos has drawn a door!'

'I haven't just drawn it,' said Cosmos huffily. 'I'm much cleverer than that you know. I've *made* you a doorway – it's a portal. It leads to—'

'Shush, Cosmos!' said Annie. She had put on her helmet again and was speaking through the voice transmitter fitted inside it. It gave her the same funny voice that had so frightened Ringo and his friends. 'Let George open it himself.'

By now George had struggled into the big heavy white suit and glass helmet that Annie had chucked

at him. Attached to the back of the suit was a small tank which fed air through a tube into the helmet so he could breathe easily inside it. He put on the big space boots and gloves that Annie had flung at him and then he stepped forward and gave the door a timid push. It flew open, revealing an enormous expanse filled with hundreds of little lights that turned out to be stars. One in particular was much bigger and brighter than the others.

'Wow!' said George, speaking through his own voice transmitter. When he'd watched *The Birth and Death of a Star*, he'd seen the events in outer space through a windowpane. But this time there didn't seem to be anything between him and outer space. It looked as though he could just step through the doorway and be there. But where? If he took that small step, where would he be?

'Where . . . ? What . . . ? How . . . ?' said George in wonder.

'See that bright star over there, the brightest star of all those you can see?' George heard Cosmos reply. 'It's the Sun. Our Sun. It looks smaller from here than when you look at it in the sky. The doorway leads to a place in the Solar System which is much further away from the Sun than Planet Earth. There is a large comet coming – that is why I have selected this location for you. You will see it in a few minutes. Please stand back from the door.'

George took a step backwards. But Annie, who was right next to him, grabbed his suit and hauled him forward again.

'Please stand back from the door, a comet is approaching,' said Cosmos as though he were announcing the arrival of a train at the station. 'Please do not stand too near the edge – the comet will be travelling at speed.'

Annie nudged George and pointed at the doorway with her foot.

'Please stand back from the door,' repeated Cosmos.

'When I count to three . . .' said Annie. She held up three fingers. Beyond the door, George could see a large rock coming towards them, much larger than the tiny one that hit the window the day before.

'This comet will not be stopping,' continued Cosmos. 'It goes straight through our Solar System.'

Annie folded one finger down to indicate 'Two'. The greyish-white rock was getting closer.

'The journey time is approximately one hundred and eighty-four years,' said Cosmos. 'Calling at Saturn, Jupiter, Mars, Earth and the Sun. On its way back it will also call at Neptune and Pluto, now out of service as a planet.'

'Please, my wonderful Cosmos, when we're out there on the comet, can you accelerate the journey? Otherwise it will take us months to see the planets!' Without waiting for Cosmos to reply, Annie shouted, '*One!*' grabbed

PLUTO

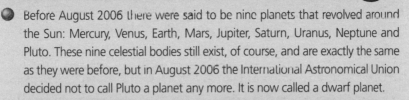

Before August 2006 there were said to be nine planets that revolved around the Sun: Mercury, Venus, Earth, Mars, Jupiter, Saturn, Uranus, Neptune and Pluto. These nine celestial bodies still exist, of course, and are exactly the same as they were before, but in August 2006 the International Astronomical Union decided not to call Pluto a planet any more. It is now called a dwarf planet.

This is due to a change in the definition of what a planet is. There now are three rules that need to be fulfilled by any object in space to be called a planet:

1) **It has to be in orbit around the Sun.**
2) **It has to be big enough for gravity to make it almost round and stay that way.**
3) **Its gravity has to have attracted almost everything that is next to it in space as it travels around the Sun, so that its path is cleared.**

According to this new definition, Pluto is not a planet any more. Is it in orbit around the Sun? Yes. Is it almost round and will it stay so? Yes. Has it cleared its path around the Sun? No: there are loads of rocks around in its orbital path. So because it failed the third rule, Pluto has been downgraded from a planet to a dwarf planet.

The other eight planets fulfil the three rules and so they remain planets. For planets and stars other than the Sun, an additional requirement has been agreed upon by the International Astronomical Union: the object should not be so big as to become a star itself at a later stage.

Planets around stars other than the Sun are called exoplanets. So far, over 240 exoplanets have been seen. Most of them are huge – much bigger than the Earth.

In December 2006 a satellite named *Corot* was sent into space. The quality of the detectors *Corot* is equipped with should allow for the discovery of exoplanets much smaller than before, down to about twice the size of the Earth. One such planet was detected using other means in 2007. It is called Gliese 581 c.

George's hand and dragged him through the doorway.

The last thing he heard was Cosmos's voice, calling as though from millions and millions of miles away, 'Don't jump! It isn't safe! Come *ba-a-a-a-ack*.'

And then there was silence.

Chapter Ten

Out in the street, Ringo and his mates were still standing there, as though stuck to the pavement by some invisible force.

'What was that?' asked a small, skinny boy who went by the name of Whippet.

'Dunno,' said the huge boy they called Tank, scratching his head.

'Well, *I* wasn't scared,' said Ringo defiantly.

'Neither was I,' chorused all the others quickly.

'I was just going to have a word with that weirdo in the spacesuit when it got frightened and ran away.'

'Yeah, yeah, yeah,' his friends all agreed hastily. 'Course you were, Ringo. Course you were.'

'So I think,' Ringo went on, '*you*' – he pointed at the newest member of his gang – 'should ring the doorbell.'

'Me?' The boy gulped.

'You said you weren't scared,' said Ringo.

'I'm not!' he squeaked.

'Then you can ring the bell, can't you?'

'Why can't you do it?' asked the new boy.

'Because I asked you first. Go on.' Ringo glared at the boy. 'Do you wanna be part of this gang?'

'Yes!' said the boy, wondering which was worse – meeting a spaceman and suffering the curse of Alien Life or making Ringo angry. He settled for the spaceman – at least he wouldn't have to see him every day at school. He edged towards Eric's front door uneasily.

'Then ring the bell, Zit,' said Ringo, 'or you'll be an *ex*-member of this gang.'

'OK,' muttered Zit, who didn't like his special new gang name much either. The others all took a few steps backwards.

The new boy's finger hovered over the bell.

'Ringo,' said one of the others suddenly, 'what're we gonna do if he opens the door?'

'*What we gonna do if he opens the door?*' Ringo

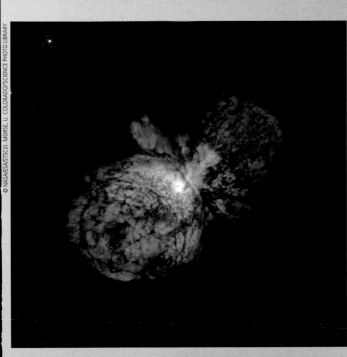

At the centre of these two giant lobes lies a star called Eta Carinae, which is about 100 times bigger than the Sun. Light takes about 8,000 years to travel from Eta Carinae to the Earth.

The Helix Nebula is a planetary nebula (a set of dust shells cast off by a star towards the end of its life). It takes about 650 years for light to travel to the Earth from the Helix Nebula.

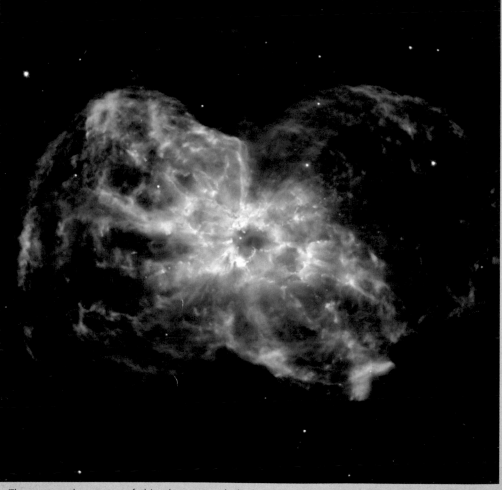

© NASA/ESA/STScI/SCIENCE PHOTO LIBRARY

The star at the centre of this planetary nebula (NGC 2440) is one of the hottest known, with a surface temperature of 200,000°C (360,000°F). As it nears the end of its life, it sheds its outer layers, creating the surrounding clouds of gas. Light takes about 4,000 years to travel from NCG 2440 to the Earth.

© JOHN THOMAS/SCIENCE PHOTO LIBRARY

In 1996, passing within 9.4 million miles (15 million km) of the Earth, Hyakutake was one of the brightest comets of the twentieth century.

© ROYAL GREENWICH OBSERVATORY/SCIENCE PHOTO LIBRARY

Halley's Comet is visible from the Earth every 76 years or so. This photo was taken in 1910.

© RICHARD J. WAINSCOAT, PETER ARNOLD INC./SCIENCE PHOTO LIBRARY

Halley's Comet in 1986.

Comet Swan is unlikely to return near the Earth again. Its path suggests it will shoot off into interstellar space, away from the Sun, for a very long time before possibly reaching another star.

On 12 January 2005, a spacecraft named *Deep Impact* was launched from Cape Canaveral, Florida, USA (right). It contained an 'impactor' (left), which was sent to hit a comet named Tempel 1, to discover what comets are made of. Comets are relics from the early Solar System, so knowing what they are made of provides information about the history of the Solar System.

Picture of comet Tempel 1 taken by the impactor as it cruised towards its target at more than 22,000 mph (36,000 km/h). The collision occurred on 4 July 2005.

1.67 seconds after the impactor hit comet Tempel 1, the *Deep Impact* spacecraft took this picture of the explosion on the surface.

The largest and most detailed true-colour image of Saturn ever produced.

The view of Saturn when seen from the Earth through a small portable telescope.

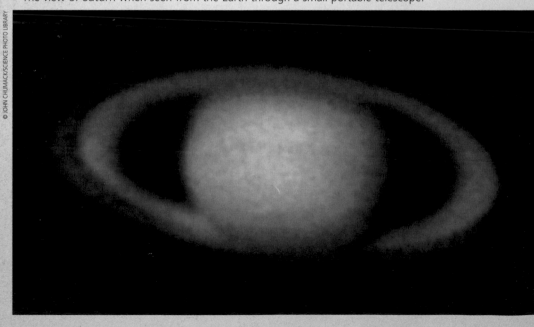

© NASA/PL/UNIVERSITY OF ARIZONA/SCIENCE PHOTO LIBRARY

Titan is the largest moon of Saturn. It is the only known moon in the Solar System to have a thick atmosphere. This is an infrared-light picture.

© NASA/JPL/SPACE SCIENCE INSTITUTE/SCIENCE PHOTO LIBRARY

Rhea is the second largest moon of Saturn. It doesn't appear to be geologically active.

© NASA/SCIENCE PHOTO LIBRARY

Iapetus is the third largest moon of Saturn. The heavily cratered region which dominates this image is known as Cassini Regio.

© NASA/SCIENCE PHOTO LIBRARY

Dione is the fourth largest moon of Saturn. Its surface is mainly composed of water ice.

© NASA/SCIENCE PHOTO LIBRARY

Tethys, the fifth largest moon of Saturn, is also probably composed of water ice.

© NASA/JPL/SPACE SCIENCE INSTITUTE/SCIENCE PHOTO LIBRARY

This is an ultraviolet, green and infrared composite image of Enceladus, the sixth largest moon of Saturn. Its surface temperature is about -200°C (-328°F), but there may be water underneath the surface.

echoed the question while he tried to think of an answer. He looked up at the sky as though searching for an idea. 'We're gonna—' Even Ringo wasn't being his usual confident, thuggish self. But before he could come up with an answer, he let out a shout of pain. 'Arrrrggghhhh!' he yelped as a hand grabbed him by the ear and twisted it quite hard.

'What,' said a stern voice, 'are you boys doing, hanging around in the street?' It was Dr Reeper – Ringo and George's class teacher from school. He had Ringo

firmly by the ear and clearly didn't intend to let go. The boys were very startled to see a teacher outside the school grounds – they never imagined that teachers actually had other lives to lead or had anywhere to go but their classrooms.

'We're not doing nothing,' squealed Ringo.

'I think you mean, "We are not doing *anything*",' corrected Dr Reeper in a teacherly voice, 'which in any case isn't true. You are obviously doing something, and if I find out that that something has been to do with bullying smaller children – like, for example, George…' Dr Reeper stared very hard at all the boys to see if any of them flinched at the mention of George's name.

'No sir no sir no sir no sir,' said Ringo, who feared his ear might come off in the teacher's hand. 'We never not touched him, we didn't. We was running after him because he . . .'

'Left-his-lunchbox-behind-at-school,' said Whippet very quickly.

'An' we wanted to give it back to him before he got home,' added Zit, the new boy.

'And did you succeed?' said Dr Reeper with a nasty smile, letting go of Ringo's ear just a little bit.

'We was just about to hand it over,' improvised Ringo, 'when he went into that house.' He pointed at Eric's front door. 'So we was ringing the bell to give it to him.'

Dr Reeper let go of Ringo's ear so suddenly that Ringo fell to the ground.

'He went in there?' Dr Reeper questioned them sharply as Ringo staggered to his feet again.

'Yeah.' They all nodded in unison.

'Why don't you boys,' said Dr Reeper slowly, 'let me have George's lunchbox and I'll hand it back to him.' He fished around in his pocket and brought out a crumpled five-pound note, which he dangled in front of their noses.

'Who's got the lunchbox?' questioned Ringo.

'Not me,' said Whippet immediately.

'Not me,' mumbled Tank.

'It must be you then,' said Ringo, pointing at Zit.

'Ringo, I haven't . . . I didn't . . . I wasn't . . .' Zit was panicking now.

'Very well,' said Dr Reeper, glaring at the four of them. He put the money back in his pocket. 'In that case, I think you'd better scram. Do you hear me? Scram!'

Once the boys – who didn't need telling twice – were gone, Dr Reeper stood in the street, smiling to himself. It wasn't a pleasant sight. Checking that no one else was coming or going, he went up to Eric's front window and squinted through it. The curtains were drawn so he only had a chink to look through. He couldn't see much, just two strangely shaped, shadowy figures which seemed to be standing near some kind of doorway inside the house.

'Interesting,' he muttered to himself. 'Very, very interesting.'

Suddenly, the temperature in the street dropped dramatically. For a second it felt as though air from the North Pole was blowing along the street. Strangely, the bitter wind seemed to be coming from under Eric's front door, but as Dr Reeper bent down to investigate, it stopped. When he went back to look through the window, the two figures had gone and there was no inside doorway to be seen.

Dr Reeper nodded to himself. 'Ah, the chill of outer space – how I long to feel it,' he whispered, rubbing his hands together. 'At last, Eric, I've found you! I knew you'd come back one day.'

Chapter Eleven

When he leaped over the threshold of the portal door, George found he was floating – not going up, not going down, just drifting in the huge great darkness of outer space. He looked back towards the doorway, but the hole in space where it should have been had closed over as though it had never been. There was no way back now and the giant rock was getting closer all the time.

'Hold my hand!' Annie shouted to George. As he gripped her hand in its space glove even harder, he started to feel as if they were falling down towards the comet. Moving faster and faster, as if they were on a giant helter-skelter, George and Annie spiralled towards the huge rock, getting closer and closer all the time. Beneath them, they could see that one side of the comet, the bit facing the Sun, was brightly lit. But the other side, which the Sun's rays didn't reach, was in darkness. Eventually they landed in a heap on a thick layer of icy dust-covered rubble. Luckily they'd come down on the bright side of the comet so they could see what lay around them.

'Ha-ha-ha-ha!'

Annie was laughing as she picked herself up. She hauled George to his feet and brushed bits of dirty ice and crumbly rock off him. 'So?' she said. 'Do you believe me now?'

'Where are we?' said George, who was so surprised he quite forgot to be scared. George felt extremely light. He looked around and saw rock, ice, snow and darkness. It was like standing on a giant dirty snowball someone had thrown into outer space. Stars blazed everywhere, their fiery glow quite different from the twinkling lights he saw from the Earth.

'We're having an adventure,' replied Annie. 'On a comet. And it's real – it isn't a made-up story, is it?'

'No, it isn't,' admitted George. He patted her spacesuit awkwardly. 'I'm sorry I didn't believe you, Annie.'

'That's all right,' said Annie generously. 'No one ever does.

That's why I had to show you. Look, George!' She waved an arm around. 'You're going to see the planets in the Solar System.' She started to pull a length of rope out of a pocket in her spacesuit.

On the end of the rope was a spike, like a tent peg. Using her space boot, she jammed the spike into the ice on the comet's surface.

Watching her, George gave a tiny little jump for joy. Even though he was wearing the spacesuit that seemed quite heavy on Earth, he couldn't believe how light he felt. So light that he thought he could leap as high as he wanted. He did another little jump across a little crack on the comet's surface. This time he went up and forward but he didn't come down again. He seemed to be taking a giant leap, maybe hundreds of metres long! He'd never be able to find Annie again . . .

'Help! Help!' George called through the helmet as his jump carried him further and further away, his arms whirling in the surrounding emptiness as he tried to make himself fall down onto the comet. But it was no good. Annie was far away in the distance now – he could only just see her when he looked back. The comet's surface was passing quickly below him. He could see holes and little hills everywhere, but nothing that he could grab on to. But at last he seemed to fall. The ground was getting closer now, and he landed and slid on the ice near the threshold between the bright and the dark side of the comet. In the distance, he saw Annie carefully running towards him.

'If you can hear me, *don't jump again*!' she was saying in a very urgent voice. 'If you can hear me, *don't jump again*! If you can—'

'*I won't!*' he called back as she reached him.

'Don't *do* that, George!' said Annie. 'You could have landed on the dark side of the comet. I might never have found you! Now stand up – the boots have small spikes on their soles.' She sounded very grown up and not at all like the impish little girl he had met at Eric's house. 'A comet is different from the Earth. We weigh much less here than we do there, so when we jump, it can take us a long, long way. This is a different world. Oh, look!' she added, changing the subject. 'We're just in time!'

'For what?' asked George.

'For *that*!' Annie pointed to the other side of the comet.

Behind the comet was a trail of ice and dust, which was getting steadily longer. As it grew, it caught the light from the faraway Sun and glistened in the wake of the comet, making it look as though thousands of diamonds were shining in outer space.

'That's beautiful,' whispered George.

For a minute he and Annie just stood there in silence.

MASS

⬡ The mass of a body measures the force needed to move it or to change the way it moves. Mass is often measured by weighing the body, but mass and weight are not the same. The weight of an object is the force attracting it to another object like the Earth or the Moon, and it depends on the mass of both objects and the distance between them. You weigh slightly less on top of a mountain because you are further from the centre of the Earth.

Earth **Moon**

Because the mass of the Moon is much less than the mass of the Earth, an astronaut who weighs about 90 kilograms (about 200 pounds) on Earth would weigh only about 15 kg (33 lbs) on the Moon. So astronauts on the Moon could, with the correct training, beat any Earth-based long-jump record.

⬡ Einstein was a German physicist who was born in 1879. He discovered that energy is equivalent to mass according to the famous equation $E=mc^2$, where 'E' is energy, 'm' is mass and 'c' is the speed of light. Because the speed of light is very large, Einstein and others realized that this equation suggested one could make an atom bomb, in which a small amount of mass is converted into a very large energy in an explosion.

⬡ Einstein also discovered that mass and energy curve space, creating gravity.

As George watched the trail grow, he realized it was made up of bits of the bright side of the comet.

'The rock's melting!' said George in a panic, clutching Annie's arm. 'What will happen when there's nothing left?'

'Don't worry.' Annie shook her head. 'We're just getting closer to the Sun. The Sun slowly warms up the bright side of the comet and the ice turns into gas. But it's OK because there's enough ice here for us to pass the Sun loads of times. Anyway, the rock under the ice won't melt. So we won't start falling through space, if that's what you're scared of.'

'I'm not scared!' protested George, letting go of her arm very suddenly. 'I was just asking.'

'Then ask more interesting questions!' said Annie.

'Like what?' asked George.

'Like, what would happen if some of the rocks from the comet's tail fell on the Earth?'

George kicked some dust around and then said reluctantly, 'All right, what would happen?'

'Now that is a good question!' said Annie, sounding pleased. 'The rocks catch fire when they enter the Earth's atmosphere and from the ground, when we look up, they become what we call shooting stars or meteors.'

They stood and gazed until the comet's tail got so long they couldn't see the end of it. But as they were watching it, the comet seemed to start changing direction: all the stars in the background were moving. 'What's happening?' George asked.

'Quick!' Annie replied. 'We've only got a few seconds. Sit down, George.' She cleared two little spaces on the ice, speedily brushing the powder

aside with her glove. Reaching into another pocket of her suit, she produced what looked like climbing hooks. 'Sit down!' she ordered again. She screwed the hooks into the ground and then fastened them onto a longish piece of cord hanging from a buckle on George's suit. 'Just in case something hits you,' she added.

'Like what?' asked George.

'Well, I don't know. My dad normally does this bit,' she replied. Next she sat down behind George and did the same to herself. 'Do you like roller coasters?' she asked him.

'I don't know,' said George, who had never been on one.

'Well, you're about to find out!' said Annie, laughing.

The comet was definitely falling – or at least changing direction towards what seemed to be 'down'. From the way the stars were moving all around him, George understood that the comet was falling very fast. But he couldn't feel anything – he didn't have butterflies in his stomach and there was no rush of air blowing past him. It wasn't at all how he had expected a ride on a roller coaster to feel. But he was starting to realize that things feel very different in outer space from the way they do on Earth.

George closed his eyes for a moment, just to see if he

COMETS

 Comets are big, dirty and not very round snowballs that travel around the Sun. They are made up of elements created in stars that exploded a long time before our Sun was born. It is believed there are more than 100 billion of them, very far away from the Sun, waiting to come closer to us. But we can only see them when they come close enough to the Sun to have a shiny trail. We have actually seen only about 1,000 comets so far.

The largest known comets have a central core of more than 20 miles (32 km) from one side to the other.

When they come close to the Sun, the ice in comets turns into gas and releases the dust that was trapped inside. This dust is probably the oldest dust there is throughout the Solar System. It contains clues about our cosmic neighbourhood at the very beginning of the life of all the planets, more than 6 billion years ago.

Most of the time, comets circle around the Sun from very far away (much, much further away than the Earth). Every now and then, one of them starts to travel towards the Sun. There are then two possibilities:

1) Some, like Halley's Comet, will get trapped by the Sun's gravity. These comets will then keep orbiting the Sun until they melt completely or until they hit a planet. Halley's Comet's core is about 9.6 miles (16 km) long. It returns near enough to the Sun to melt down a bit and have a trail that can be seen by us about every 76 years. It was near us in 1986 and will be back in 2061. Some of the comets trapped by the Sun's gravity return near the Sun much more rarely. The Hyakutake Comet, for instance, will travel for 110,000 years before coming back.

2) Because they have too much speed or because they do not travel close enough to the Sun, some other comets, like Comet Swan, never come back. They pass by us once and then start an immense journey in outer space towards another star. These comets are cosmic wanderers. Their interstellar journey can take hundreds of thousands of years, sometimes less, sometimes even more.

could feel anything at all. But no, nothing. Suddenly, with his eyes closed, he realized, that something in space must be pulling them and the comet towards it for the comet to change direction like that. George instinctively knew that this something was probably much, much bigger than the comet on which he and Annie were surfing through outer space.

Chapter Twelve

When George opened his eyes again, he saw a massive pale-yellow planet with a belt of rings rising in the dark sky ahead of them. They sped along on the comet, heading for a point just above the rings. From far away, the rings looked like soft ribbons. Some were pale yellow, like the planet itself; others were darker.

'This is Saturn,' said Annie. 'And I saw it first.'

'I know what it is!' replied George. 'And what do you mean first? I'm in front of you. *I* saw it first!'

'No, you weren't looking, you were too scared! You had your eyes shut!' Annie's voice rang inside his helmet.

'*Ner*-ner-na-*ner-ner*.'

'No I didn't!' protested George.

'Shhh!' Annie interrupted him. 'Did you know that Saturn is the second biggest of the planets that move around the Sun?'

'Of course I knew,' lied George.

'Oh really?' replied Annie. 'Then if you knew that, you'll know which is the biggest planet of all.'

'Well . . . er . . .' said George, who had no idea. 'It's the Earth, isn't it?'

'*Wrong!*' trumpeted Annie. 'The Earth is teeny-weeny, just like your silly little brain. The Earth is only number five.'

'How do you know that?'

'How do I know you've got a silly little brain?' said Annie cheekily.

'No, stupid,' said George furiously. 'How do you know about the planets?'

'Because I've done this trip many, many times before,' said Annie, tossing her head as though throwing back her ponytail. 'So let me tell you. And listen carefully,' she ordered. 'There are eight planets orbiting the Sun. Four are huge and four are small. The huge ones are Jupiter, Saturn, Neptune and Uranus. But the two biggest are so much bigger than the others that they are called the Giants. Saturn is the second of the Giant Planets, and the biggest one of all is Jupiter. The four small planets are Mars, Earth, Venus and Mercury,' she continued, ticking them off on her fingers. 'The Earth is the biggest of the small ones, but if you put these four together into a ball, you still wouldn't get anything nearly as big as Saturn. Saturn is more than forty-five times bigger than these four small planets added together.'

Annie was clearly delighted to be showing off about the planets. Even though he was very annoyed by how smug she was, George was secretly impressed. All he had ever done was dig potatoes and mess around with a pig in his back garden. It wasn't much in comparison with riding around the Solar System on a comet.

As Annie talked, the comet flew nearer and nearer to Saturn. They got so close that George could see that the rings were made not of ribbons but of ice, rocks and stones. These were all different sizes, the smallest no bigger than a speck of dust, the largest about four metres long. Most of them were moving much too fast for George to catch one. But then he spotted a small chunk of rock calmly floating right next to him. A quick glance behind showed that Annie wasn't looking. He reached out, snatched up the rock and held it in his space glove! A real treasure from outer space! His heart was beating fast. The sound was so loud in his ears that he thought Annie must be able to hear it through the sound transmitter in his helmet. He suspected that taking

things home from outer space was probably not allowed so he hoped she hadn't noticed.

'George, are you all right?' asked Annie. 'Why are you wriggling around like that?'

George quickly thought of something to say to divert her attention from the rock he was trying to stuff into his pocket.

THE SOLAR SYSTEM

- The Solar System is the cosmic family of our Sun. It comprises all the objects trapped by the Sun's gravity: planets, dwarf planets, moons, comets, asteroids and other small objects yet to be discovered. An object trapped by the Sun's gravity is said to be in orbit around the Sun.
- Closest planet to the Sun: Mercury
- Mercury is 36 million miles (57.9 million km) away from the Sun on average.
- Furthest planet from the Sun: Neptune
  Neptune is 2.8 billion miles (4.5 billion km) away from the Sun on average.

> Distance of the Earth from the Sun: 93 million miles (149.6 million km) on average.

- Number of planets: 8
- From closest to the Sun, the planets are: Mercury, Venus, Earth, Mars, Jupiter, Saturn, Uranus and Neptune

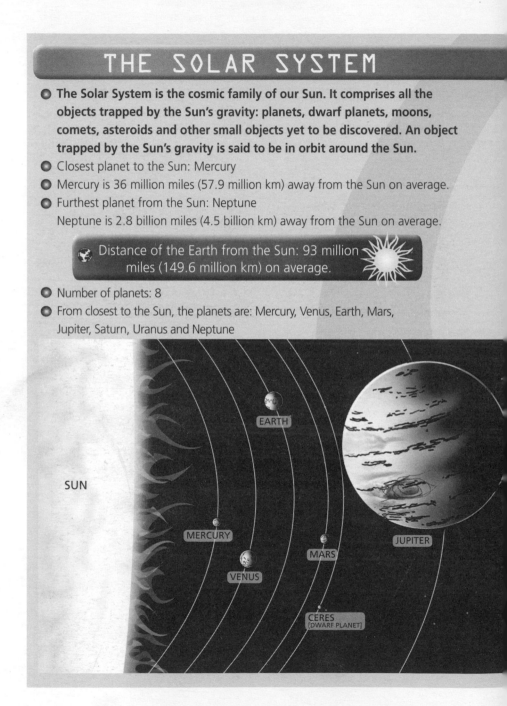

SUN

EARTH

MERCURY

VENUS

MARS

JUPITER

CERES
[DWARF PLANET]

- Number of dwarf planets: 3
- From closest to furthest to the Sun, the dwarf planets are: Ceres, Pluto and Eris
- Number of known planetary moons: 165
  Mercury: 0; Venus: 0; Earth: 1; Mars: 2; Jupiter: 63;
  Saturn: 59; Uranus: 27; Neptune: 13
- Number of known comets: 1,000 (estimated real number:1,000,000,000,000,000)

Furthest distance travelled by a man-made object: more than
9.3 billion miles (14.96 billion km). 9.3 billion miles is the
distance reached by *Voyager 1* on 15 August 2006 at 10.13
a.m. (Greenwich Mean Time). This corresponds to exactly 100
times the distance from the Earth to the Sun. *Voyager 1* is still
travelling away.

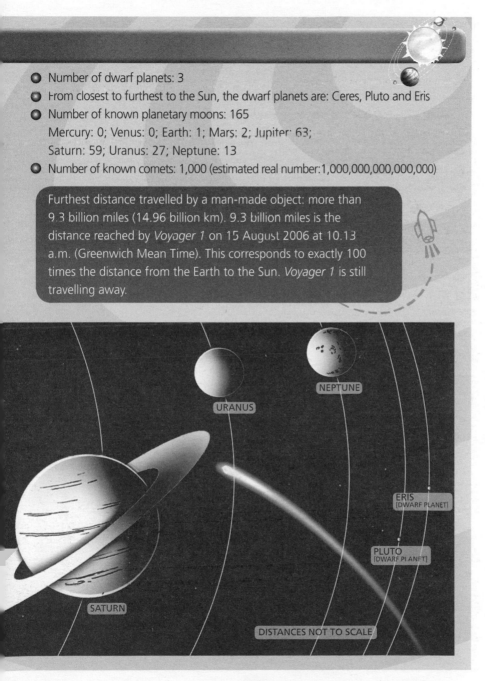

NEPTUNE

URANUS

ERIS
[DWARF PLANET]

PLUTO
[DWARF PLANET]

SATURN

DISTANCES NOT TO SCALE

'Why did we change direction? Why did our comet move towards Saturn? Why didn't we continue straight on?' he gabbled.

'Oh dear, you just don't know anything at all, do you?' sighed Annie. 'It's lucky for you that I'm such a fount of useful scientific knowledge,' she added importantly. 'We moved towards Saturn because we fell towards it. Just like an apple falls on Earth; just like we fell onto the comet when we arrived; just like the particles in space clouds fall onto each other and become balls that become stars. Everything falls towards everything throughout the Universe. And do you know the name of what causes this fall?'

George didn't have a clue.

'It's called gravity.'

'So it's because of gravity that we're going to fall on Saturn now? And crash?'

'No, silly! We're moving way too fast to crash. We're just flying by to say hello.'

Annie waved to Saturn and shouted, *'Hello, Saturn!'* so loudly that George's hands automatically tried to cover his ears, but he couldn't because of his helmet, so instead he yelled back, *'Don't shout!'*

'Oh, I'm sorry,' she said. 'I didn't mean to.'

As they whizzed past Saturn, George saw that Annie was right – the comet didn't fall all the way onto the giant planet but cruised straight past it. With a bit of distance now, he could see that Saturn not only had

rings, but also a moon, like the Earth. Looking closer, he could hardly believe his eyes! He saw another moon, and another and yet another! In total, he saw five large moons and even more small ones before Saturn was too far away for him to keep counting. *Saturn has at least five moons!* he thought. George hadn't known

SATURN

- Saturn is the sixth closest planet to the Sun.
- Average distance to the Sun: 888 million miles (1,430 million km)
- Diameter at equator: 74,898 miles (120,536 km) corresponding to 9.449 diameters at equator on Earth
- Surface area: 83.7 x Earth's surface area
- Volume: 763.59 x Earth's volume
- Mass: 95 x Earth's mass
- Gravity at the equator: 91.4% of Earth's gravity at Earth's equator.

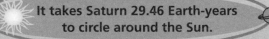

It takes Saturn 29.46 Earth-years to circle around the Sun.

- Structure: Hot rocky core that is surrounded by a liquid metal layer which is itself surrounded by a liquid hydrogen and helium layer. There then is an atmosphere that surrounds it all.

- Winds have been recorded at speeds up to 1,116 mph (1,795 km/h) in Saturn's atmosphere. By comparison, the strongest wind ever recorded on Earth is 231 mph (371.68 km/h) at Mount Washington, New Hampshire, USA, on 12 April 1934. It is believed that wind speeds can sometimes reach over 300 mph (480 km/h) inside tornadoes. However devastating these are, these winds are still very slow compared to Saturn's winds.

So far, Saturn has 59 confirmed moons. Seven of them are round. Titan, the largest, is the only known moon within the Solar System to have an atmosphere. In volume, Titan is more than three times bigger than our Moon.

that a planet other than the Earth could have even one moon, let alone five! He looked at Saturn with respect as the giant planet with rings shrank into the distance behind them until it was just a bright dot in the starry background.

Chapter Thirteen

The comet was now travelling straight again. In front of them, the Sun was bigger and brighter than before, but still quite small compared to its size when seen from the Earth. George spotted another bright dot that he hadn't noticed before, a dot that was quickly growing bigger as they approached it.

'What's over there?' he asked, pointing ahead and to the right. 'Is that another planet?'

But there was no reply. When he looked round, Annie had gone. George untied himself from the comet and followed the trail of footprints she had left in the icy powder. He carefully gauged the length of his steps so that he wouldn't find himself flying off the comet again.

After climbing gingerly over a small icy hill, he saw her. She was peering into a hole in the ground. Around the hole were bits and pieces of rock which seemed to have been spat out by the comet itself. George walked over and looked down into the hole too. It was a metre or so deep, with nothing much to be seen at the bottom.

'What is it?' he asked. 'Have you found something?'

'Well, you see, I went for a walk—' Annie started to explain.

'Why didn't you say?' George interrupted her.

'You were shouting at me about not shouting!' said Annie. 'So I thought I'd just go by myself. Because then there'd be no one to get *cross* with me,' she added pointedly.

'I'm not *cross* with you,' said George.

'Yes you are! You're always cross with me. It doesn't make any difference if I'm nice to you or not.'

'*I'm not cross!*' shouted George.

'*Yes you are!*' shouted back Annie, balling her gloved hands into fists and shaking them at George. As she did so, something extraordinary happened. A little fountain of gas and dirt blew up from the ground just next to her.

'Now look what you've done!' complained George. But as he spoke, another little fountain erupted through the rock right next to him. It formed a cloud of dust that slowly dispersed.

'Annie, what's happening?' he asked.

'Um, it's nothing,' replied Annie. 'This is all fine, don't

worry.' But she didn't sound very sure. 'Why don't we go and sit down where we were before?' she suggested. 'It's nicer over there.'

But as they walked back, more and more little geysers of dust erupted around them, leaving a haze of smoke in the air. Neither of them felt very safe but neither of them wanted to admit it. They just walked more and more quickly towards the place where they'd been sitting before. Without saying a word, they anchored themselves to the comet once more.

In the sky, the bright dot George had seen growing had become much bigger. It now looked like a planet with red and blue stripes.

'That's Jupiter,' Annie said, breaking the silence. But she was whispering now. She didn't sound like the confident show-off she had been earlier. 'It's the biggest of the planets, about twice the volume of Saturn. That makes it more than a thousand times the volume of Earth.'

'Does Jupiter have moons too?' George asked.

'Yes, it does,' replied Annie. 'But I don't know how many. I didn't count them last time I was here so I'm not sure.'

'Have you really been here before?' George looked suspicious.

'Of course I have!' said Annie indignantly. George wasn't sure he believed her.

Once again, the comet and Annie and George started

to fall. As they fell, George gazed at Jupiter. Even by Saturn's standards, Jupiter was enormous.

As they flew by, Annie pointed out a big red mark on Jupiter's surface.

'That thing,' she said, 'is a huge storm. It's been going on for hundreds and hundreds of years. Maybe even more, I don't know. It's over twice the size of the Earth!'

As they moved away from Jupiter, George counted how many moons he could spot.

'Four big ones,' he said.

'Four big ones what?'

'Moons. Jupiter has four big moons and lots and lots of little moons. I think it has even more moons than Saturn.'

'Oh, OK,' said Annie, who was sounding nervous now. 'If you say so.'

George was worried – it wasn't like Annie to agree with anything he said. He noticed she had shuffled a little closer to him and slipped her hand in its space glove into his. All around them, new jets of gas and dust were springing up out of the rock, each one spitting out a small cloud. A thin haze was forming over the whole comet. 'Are you all right?' he asked Annie. She had stopped showing off and being rude, and he felt sure something was very wrong.

'George, I—' Annie started to reply when a huge rock smashed into the comet behind them, shaking the ground like an earthquake and sending up even more dust and ice into the haze.

Looking up, George and Annie saw there were hundreds and hundreds of rocks, all coming towards them at high speed. And there was nowhere to hide.

'Asteroids!' cried Annie. 'We're in an asteroid storm!'

JUPITER

- Jupiter is the fifth closest planet to the Sun.
- Average distance to the Sun: 483.6 million miles (778.3 million km)
- Diameter at equator: 88,846 miles (142,984 km), corresponding to 11.209 diameters at equator on Earth
- Surface area: 120.5 x Earth's surface area
- Volume: 1,321.3 x Earth's volume
- Mass: 317.8 x Earth's mass
- Gravity at the equator: 236% of Earth's gravity at Earth's equator
- Structure: Small (compared to the overall size of the planet) rocky core surrounded by a liquid metal layer which smoothly turns into a liquid hydrogen layer as height increases. This liquid then smoothly turns into an atmosphere made of hydrogen gas that surrounds it all. Even though it is bigger, Jupiter's overall composition is similar to Saturn's.

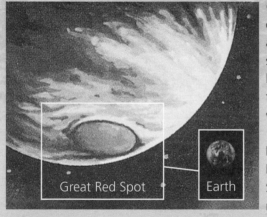

Great Red Spot

Earth

- The Great Red Spot on Jupiter's surface is a giant hurricane-type storm, a hurricane that has lasted for more than three centuries (it was first observed in 1655), but it may have been there for even longer. The Great Red Spot storm is huge: more than twice the size of the Earth. Winds on Jupiter often reach 620 mph (1,000 km/h).
- It takes Jupiter 11.86 Earth-years to circle around the Sun.
- So far, Jupiter has 63 confirmed moons. Four of them are big enough to be round and were seen by the Italian scientist Galileo in 1610. These are collectively known as the Galilean moons. They are: Io, Europa, Ganymede and Callisto, and are about the same size as our Moon.

Chapter Fourteen

'What do we do?' yelled George.

'Nothing,' shrieked Annie. 'There's nothing we *can* do! Try not to get squashed! I'll call Cosmos to get us back.'

The comet shot through the asteroids incredibly fast. Another large rock hit the comet just in front of them, raining down smaller rocks on their spacesuits and helmets. Through the voice transmitter in his helmet, George heard Annie scream. But suddenly the scream went silent – the noise just stopped like a radio being switched off.

George tried to say something to Annie through the voice transmitter but she didn't seem to hear him. He turned to look at her – he could see she was trying to speak to him from inside the glass space helmet, but he couldn't hear anything she said. He shouted as loudly as he could: '*Annie! Get us home! Get us home!*' But it was no use. He could see now that the tiny antenna on her helmet was snapped in half. That must be why he couldn't talk to her! Did this mean she couldn't talk to Cosmos either?

Annie was nodding madly and holding onto George very tightly. She was trying as hard as she could to summon Cosmos to come and get them both but the computer wasn't answering. As George feared, the device that linked her both to him and to Cosmos had been broken by the rocks raining down on them. They were stuck on the comet, flying through an asteroid storm, and it seemed there was no way out. George tried to call Cosmos himself but he didn't know how to do it or whether he even had the right equipment. He got no reply. Annie and George hung onto each other and squeezed their eyes shut.

But just as suddenly as the storm had started, it stopped again. One minute rocks were thudding down on the comet all around them, the next the comet had flown out of the other side of the storm. Looking around, George and Annie realized how very lucky they had been to escape. The rocks were forming a huge line

that seemed to extend all the way through space. They were mainly large and scattered thinly along the line, except where the comet had flown through. The rocks here were much smaller but more densely packed.

However, they were still far, far from safe. Jets of gas from the comet were now shooting out everywhere. Soon one could erupt right underneath them. It was now so hazy from all the explosions that they could hardly see the sky. Just the Sun and a faint little blue dot that was slowly getting bigger.

George turned back to Annie and pointed at the blue dot ahead. She nodded and tried to spell out a word with the finger of her space glove in the air. George could only make out the first letter – E. As they got closer to it, the comet tilted slightly towards it and George suddenly realized what Annie was trying to tell him. It was E for Earth! The tiny blue dot in front of him was the planet Earth. It was so small compared to the other

ASTEROID BELT

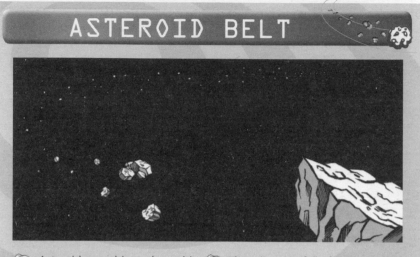

Asteroids are objects that orbit the Sun but are not big enough to be round and to be called planets or dwarf planets. There are millions of them around the Sun: 5,000 new asteroids are discovered every month. Their size varies from rocks a few inches across up to several hundred miles wide.

There is a ring full of asteroids that circle the Sun. This ring lies between Mars and Jupiter. It is called the Asteroid Belt. Even though there are a lot of asteroids in the Asteroid Belt, it is so huge and spread out that most of the asteroids there are lone space travellers. Some places, however, may be more crowded than others.

planets, and so beautiful. And it was his planet and his home. He desperately wanted to be back there now, this very second. He wrote 'Cosmos' in the air with his space glove. But Annie just shook her head and wrote the word 'NO' with her finger.

Around them on the comet conditions were getting worse by the second. Hundreds and hundreds of fountains of gas and dust were erupting all over it. They huddled together, two castaways in space, with no idea how to get out of the awful trouble they had landed themselves in.

At least, George thought, in a strange dreamlike way, *I've seen the Earth from space*. And he wished he could have told everyone back home how tiny and fragile the Earth was compared to the other planets. But there was no way they could get back home now. The fog of dust and gas was now so thick that they had even lost sight of the Earth's blue colour. How could Cosmos have let them down like this?

George was just wondering if this was the last thought he'd ever have when suddenly a doorway filled with light appeared on the ground next to them. Through it came a man in a spacesuit, who unhooked them both from the comet and, one by one, picked them up and threw them through the door. A split second later, Annie and then George landed with a bump on the floor of Eric's library. The man who had grabbed them quickly followed and the doorway slammed shut behind him. Pulling off his space helmet and glaring down at George and Annie, who were sprawled on the library floor in their spacesuits, Eric shouted:

'*What on Earth did you think you were doing?!*'

Chapter Fifteen

'*What on Earth did you think you were doing?!*'
Eric was so angry that, for a moment, George wished he were still on the roller-coaster comet, heading straight for the heart of the Sun.

'Actually, we weren't on the Earth,' murmured Annie, who was struggling out of her suit.

'*I heard that!*' Eric rounded on her. George hadn't thought Eric could get any angrier than he already was, but now he looked so furious George thought he might explode. He half expected to see great jets of steam burst out of his ears, just like the ones on the comet.

'Go to your room, Annie,' ordered Eric. 'I'll talk to you later.'

'But Da-ddee . . .' Annie began. But even she fell silent under Eric's glare. She pulled off her heavy space boots, wriggled out of her suit and shot out of the door like a streak of blonde lightning. 'Bye, George,' she muttered as she legged it past him.

'As for you . . .' said Eric in such a menacing tone that George's blood ran cold. But then he realized Eric wasn't talking to him. He was looming over Cosmos, casting threatening looks at the computer screen.

'Master,' said Cosmos mechanically, 'I am just a humble machine. I can only obey the commands I am given.'

'Stuff and nonsense!' cried Eric wildly. 'You are the world's most powerful computer! You let two children travel into outer space by themselves – if I hadn't come home when I did, who knows what might have happened? You could have – you *should* have – stopped them!'

'Oh dear, I think I am about to crash,' replied Cosmos, and his screen suddenly went blank.

Eric clutched his head in his hands and staggered about the room for a minute. 'I can't believe this,' he said, as though to himself. 'Terrible, terrible!' He groaned loudly. 'What a disaster!'

'I'm very sorry,' said George timidly.

Eric whipped round and stared at him. 'I trusted you, George,' he said. 'I would never have showed you Cosmos if I'd thought that the minute my back was turned, you would sneak through the doorway into outer space like that. And taking a younger child with you! You have no idea how dangerous it is out there.'

George wanted to cry out that this was so unfair! It wasn't his fault – it was Annie who had pushed them both through the doorway into outer space, not him. But he kept quiet. Annie, he figured, was in enough trouble already without him making it worse.

'There are things in outer space you can't even imagine,' continued Eric. 'Extraordinary, fascinating, enormous, amazing things. But dangerous. So dangerous. I was going to tell you all about them, but now . . .' He shook his head. 'I'm going to take you home.' And then Eric said a dreadful thing. 'I need to have a word with your parents.'

As George found out afterwards, Eric had more than just one word with his parents. In fact, he had quite a few, enough to make them feel very disappointed in their son. They were very hurt that despite all their good intentions about bringing up George to love nature and hate technology, he'd been caught red-handed at Eric's house playing with a computer. A valuable and delicate one as well; one that wasn't for kids to touch. Worse, George had invented some kind of game (Eric had become rather vague at this point), which he'd persuaded Annie to join in, and this game had been very dangerous and very silly. As a result, the two children were both grounded and not allowed to play together for a whole month.

'Huh, good!' said George when his dad told him what his punishment would be. At that moment he never wanted to see Annie again. She'd got him into so much trouble already, and yet George had been the one to take all the blame.

'And,' added George's dad, who was looking very cross and bristly today with his big bushy beard and his itchy, hairy home-made shirt, 'Eric has promised me he will keep his computer locked up so neither of you will be able to get near it.'

'*No-o-o!*' cried George. 'He can't do that!'

'Oh yes he can,' said George's dad very severely. 'And he will.'

'But Cosmos will get lonely all by himself!' said George, too upset to realize what he was saying.

'George,' said his dad, looking worried, 'you do understand that this is a computer and not a living being we're talking about? Computers can't get lonely – they don't have feelings.'

'But this one does!' shouted George.

'Oh dear,' sighed his dad. 'If this is the effect that technology has on you, you see how right we are to keep you away from it.'

George ground his teeth in frustration at the way adults twisted everything to make it sound like they were always right, and then dragged his feet up the stairs to his room. The world suddenly seemed a much more boring place.

George knew he was going to miss Cosmos but what he didn't expect was that he would miss Annie too. At first he was pleased to be banned from seeing her – it was good to have a punishment that stopped him from doing something he didn't want to do anyway. But after a while he found himself looking out for the flash of her golden hair. He told himself he was just bored. He was grounded, so he couldn't go and see any of his other friends, and there wasn't much for him to do at home that was any fun – his mum wanted him to weave a rug for his bedroom and his dad attempted to get him interested in his home-made electricity generator. George tried to be enthusiastic but he felt rather flat.

The only bright star in his life was that he'd seen a poster at school advertising a science presentation competition – the first prize was a computer! George desperately wanted to win. He spent ages trying to write a really good talk about the wonders of the Universe and drawing pictures of the planets he'd seen on the comet

ride. But no matter how hard he tried, he just couldn't seem to get the words right. Everything sounded wrong. Eventually he gave up in frustration and resigned himself to a boring life for ever and ever.

But then at last something interesting happened. One grey autumn afternoon at the end of October – the slowest and dullest month he had ever lived through – George was mooching about in the back garden when he noticed something unusual. Through a small round hole in the fence he saw something very blue. He went over to it and pressed his eye-socket to the fence. From the other side he heard a squeak.

'George!' said a familiar voice. He was eye to eye with Annie.

'We're not supposed to be talking to each other,' he whispered through the fence.

'I know!' she said. 'But I'm so bored.'

'You're bored! But you've got Cosmos!'

'No I haven't,' said Annie. 'My dad has locked him up so I can't play with him any more.' She sniffed. 'I'm not even allowed to go Trick or Treating for Halloween this evening.'

'Me neither,' said George.

'I've got such a lovely witch's costume too,' said Annie sadly.

'My mum's making pumpkin pie for supper right now,' George told her glumly. 'I bet it'll be horrible. And when she's finished, I'll have to go and eat a slice of it in the kitchen.'

'Pumpkin pie!' said Annie longingly. 'That sounds really nice. Can I have your slice if you don't want it?'

'Yeah, but you're not allowed in my kitchen, are you? After what happened . . . last time we played together.'

'I'm really sorry,' said Annie. 'About the comet ride and the asteroids and the jets of gas and my dad getting cross with you. And everything. I didn't mean it.'

George didn't reply. He'd thought of so many angry things to say to Annie but now that he was nearly face to face with her, he didn't feel like saying any of them.

'Oh dear,' sniffed Annie.

From the other side of the fence, George thought he heard the noise of crying. 'Annie?' he called quietly. 'Annie?'

Brrreeeewwwhhh! George heard a sound like someone furiously blowing their nose.

He ran down the length of the fence. His dad had started to mend the hole where Freddy had broken through into Next Door but he'd got distracted halfway through and had forgotten to finish the job. There was still a little gap, maybe large enough for a small person to squeeze through.

'Annie!' George poked his head through the space. He could see her on the other side now, wiping her nose on her sleeve and rubbing her eyes. Wearing normal clothes, she no longer looked like a strange fairy child or a visitor from outer space. She just looked like a lonely little girl. Suddenly George felt really sorry for her. 'Come on!' he said. 'Climb through! We can hide together in Freddy's sty.'

'But I thought you hated me!' said Annie, scampering down to the hole in the fence. 'Because of—'

'Oh, that!' said George carelessly, as though he'd never given it a moment's thought. 'When I was a little kid, I *would* have minded,' he said grandly. 'But I don't now.'

'Oh,' said Annie, whose face was blurred by tears. 'So can we be friends?'

'Only if you climb through the fence,' teased George.

'But what about your dad?' asked Annie doubtfully. 'Won't he be cross again?'

'He's gone out,' said George. 'He won't be back for hours.' In fact, that morning George had been rather pleased to be grounded. Sometimes on Saturdays his dad often took George with him when he went on global-warming protest marches. When he was younger, George had loved the marches – he'd thought that walking through the centre of town carrying a placard and shouting slogans was great fun. The eco-warriors were very jolly and sometimes they would give George piggy-back rides or mugs of steaming home-made soup But now that George was older, he found going on marches a bit embarrassing. So when his dad had sternly told him

that morning that, as part of his ongoing punishment, he would have to miss that day's protest march and stay at home, George pretended to be sad so as not to hurt his dad's feelings. But secretly he had breathed a sigh of relief.

'Come on, Annie, jump through,' he said.

The pigsty wasn't the warmest or the most comfortable place to sit but it was the one best hidden from angry grown-up eyes. George thought Annie might protest at the smell of pig – which wasn't as strong as people tended to think – but she just wrinkled her nose and then snuggled down in some straw in the corner. Freddy was asleep, his warm breath coming out in little piggy snores as he dozed, his big head resting on his trotters.

'So, no more adventures then?' George asked Annie, settling down next to her.

'Not likely,' said Annie, scuffing her trainers against the pigsty wall. 'Dad says I can't go into outer space again until I'm really old, like twenty-three or something.'

'Twenty-three? But that's ages!'

'I know,' sighed Annie. 'It's for ever away. But at least he didn't tell my mum. She would have been *really* cross. I promised her I'd look after Dad and stop him doing anything silly.'

'Where is your mum anyway?' asked George.

'My mum,' said Annie, tilting her head in a way he had come to recognize, 'is dancing *Swan Lake* with the Bolshoi Ballet in Moscow.'

In his sleep, Freddy gave a loud snort.

'No she isn't,' said George. 'Even Freddy knows that's not true.'

'Oh all right,' agreed Annie. 'She's looking after Granny, who isn't very well.'

'Then why didn't you say so?'

'Because it's much more interesting to say something

else. But it was true about outer space, wasn't it?'

'Yes, it was,' said George. 'And it was truly amazing. But . . .' He paused.

'What?' said Annie, who was making a plait out of Freddy's straw.

'Why does your dad go there? I mean, why does he have Cosmos? What's he for?'

''Cos he's trying to find a new planet in the Universe.'

'What sort of new planet?' asked George.

'A special one. One where people could live. Y'know, in case the Earth gets too hot.'

'Wow! Has he found one?'

'Not yet,' said Annie. 'But he keeps looking and looking, everywhere across all the galaxies in the Universe. He can't stop until he finds one.'

'That's amazing. I wish I had a computer that could take me across the whole Universe. Actually, I wish I had a computer at all.'

'You don't have a computer?' Annie sounded surprised. 'Why not?'

'I'm saving up for one. But it's going to take years and years and years.'

'That's not much good, is it?'

'So,' said George, 'I'm entering a science competition and the first prize is a computer, a really huge one!'

'What competition?'

'It's a science presentation. You have to give a talk. And the person who does the best one wins the computer. Lots of schools are taking part.'

'Oh, I know!' said Annie, sounding excited. 'I'm going to it with my school – it's next week, isn't it? I'm staying at Granny's all next week so I'm going to school from there. But I'll see you at the competition.'

'Are you entering?' George asked, suddenly worried that Annie, with her interesting life, scientific know-how and vivid imagination, would pull off a presentation that made his own sound about as thrilling as cold rice pudding.

'No, course not!' said Annie. 'I don't want to win a stupid computer. If it was some ballet shoes, then that would be different . . . What are you going to talk about?'

'Well,' said George shyly, 'I've been trying to write something about the Solar System. But I don't think it's very good. I don't know very much about it.'

'Yes you do!' said Annie. 'You know loads more than

anyone else at school does. You've actually seen parts of the Solar System, like Saturn, Jupiter, asteroids and even the Earth from outer space!'

'But what if I've got it all wrong?'

'Why don't you get Dad to check it for you?' suggested Annie.

'He's so cross with me,' said George sadly. 'He won't want to help me.'

'I'll ask him this evening,' said Annie firmly. 'And then you can come round after school on Monday and talk to him.'

At that moment there was a gentle tap on the roof. The two children both froze as the door to the pigsty swung open.

'Hello?' said a nice voice.

'It's my mum!' George mouthed silently to Annie.

'Oh no!' she mouthed back.

'Trick or treat?' said George's mum.

'Treat?' said George hopefully. Annie nodded.

'Treat for two?'

'Yes please,' replied George. 'For me and, er, Freddy, that is.'

'Freddy's a funny name for a girl,' said George's mum.

'Oh please, George's mum!' Annie burst out. She couldn't stay silent any longer. 'Don't let George get into more trouble! It isn't his fault!'

'Don't you worry,' said George's mum in the sort of voice that they both knew meant she was smiling.

'I think it's silly you can't play together. I've brought you both your tea – some nice broccoli muffins and a slice of pumpkin pie!'

With a squeak of delight, Annie fell on the plateful of lumpy, funny-shaped buns. 'Thank you!' she mumbled through a mouthful of muffin. 'These are delicious!'

Chapter Sixteen

eanwhile, on the other side of town, George's dad was having a lovely time on his eco-march. Holding up huge placards and shouting slogans, the campaigners charged across the shopping precinct, batting the crowds aside. '*The planet is dying!*' they cried as they marched to the market square. '*Recycle plastic bags! Ban the car!*' they bellowed to surprised passers-by. '*Stop wasting the Earth's resources!*' they yelled.

When they reached the middle of the square, George's dad jumped up onto the base of a statue to give a speech.

'*Now* is the time to start worrying! Not tomorrow!' he began. No one heard him so one of his friends handed him a megaphone. '*We don't have that many years left to save the planet!*' he repeated, this time so loudly that everyone in the area could hear him. 'If the Earth's temperature continues to rise,' he went on, 'by the end of the century, flood and droughts will kill thousands and force over two hundred million people to flee from their homes. Much of the world will become uninhabitable. Food production will collapse and people will starve. Technology will not be able to save us. *Because it will be too late!*'

A few people in the crowd were clapping and nodding their heads. George's dad felt quite surprised. He'd been coming on these marches for years and years, handing out flyers and giving speeches. He'd got quite used to people ignoring him or telling him he was crazy because he believed that people owned too many cars, caused too much pollution and relied too heavily on energy-consuming machines. And now, suddenly,

people were listening to the eco-horror story he'd been talking about for so long.

'The polar ice-caps are melting, the seas are rising, the climate is getting warmer and warmer,' he went on. 'The advances in science and technology have given us the power to destroy our planet! Now we need to work out how to save it!'

By now, a little group of Saturday shoppers had stopped to hear what he had to say. A small cheer went up from the people listening.

'*It's time to save our planet!*' cried George's dad.

'*Save our planet!*' the campaigners shouted back at him, one or two of the shoppers joining in. '*Save our planet! Save our planet!*'

As a few more people cheered, George's dad lifted his arms in the air in a victory salute. He felt very excited.

At last people were taking some notice of the terrible state the planet was in. He suddenly realized that all those years he had spent trying to raise public awareness were not lost after all. It was starting to work. All the eco-friendly groups had not protested in vain. When the cheers tailed off, George's dad was about to speak again when suddenly, out of nowhere, a huge custard pie sailed across the heads of the crowd and hit him right in the face.

There was a moment of shocked silence, and then everyone burst out laughing at the sight of poor George's dad standing there, with runny cream dripping down his beard. Wriggling through the onlookers, a group of boys dressed in Halloween costumes started running away from the market square.

'Catch them!' shouted someone in the crowd, pointing to the band of masked figures sprinting away as fast as they could, laughing their heads off as they went.

George's dad didn't really mind – after all, people had

been throwing things at him for years while he made his speeches; he'd been arrested, jostled, insulted and thrown out of so many places in his efforts to make people understand the danger the planet faced, that one more custard pie didn't upset him very much. He just wiped the sticky goo out of his eyes and got ready to carry on talking.

A few of the other green campaigners ran after the group of demons, devils and zombies, but they were soon left behind, staggering and gasping for breath.

When the boys realized that the grown-ups had given up the chase, they came to a halt.

'Ha-ha-ha-ha,' sniggered one of them, ripping off his zombie mask to reveal the features of Ringo beneath. His real face wasn't much more attractive than the rubber mask.

'That was brilliant!' gasped Whippet, stripping off his

black and white *Scream* mask. 'The way you threw that pie, Ringo!'

'Yeah!' agreed an enormous devil, swishing his tail and waving his trident. 'You got him right on the nose, you did!' Judging by his great size, it could be none other than Tank, the boy who just couldn't stop growing.

'I love Halloween,' said Ringo happily. 'No one will ever know it was us!'

'What shall we do next?' squeaked Zit, who was dressed as Dracula.

'Well, we've run outta pies,' said Ringo. 'So we're going to play some *tricks* now, some good ones. I've got some ideas . . .'

By late that afternoon the boys had given quite a few people living in their small town a nasty fright. They'd shot an old lady with coloured water from a toy pistol, they'd thrown purple flour over a group of small kids and let off fire crackers under a parked car, making its owner think they'd blown it up. Each time, they had caused as much havoc as possible and then scampered away very quickly before anyone could catch them.

Now they had reached the edge of town, where the houses started to spread out. Instead of narrow streets with rows of snug little cottages, the buildings got bigger and further apart. These houses had long green lawns in front of them, with big hedges and crunchy gravel driveways. It was getting dark, and some of these enormous houses, with their blank windows, columns and grand front doors, were starting to look quite eerie in the dim light. Most of them were dark and silent so the gang didn't even bother ringing their bells. They were just about to give up for the day when they came to the very last house in the town, a huge rambling place with turrets, crumbling statues and old iron gates hanging off their hinges. On the ground floor, lights were blazing from every window.

'Last one!' announced Ringo cheerfully. 'So let's make it a good one. Tricks at the ready?'

His band of boys checked their stash of trick weapons

and hurried along behind him up the weed-covered driveway. But as they approached the house, they all noticed a strange eggy smell, which grew stronger as they approached the front door.

'Pooo-eeey!' said the huge devil, holding his nose. 'Who did that?'

'Wasn't me!' squawked Zit.

'He who smelt it dealt it,' said Ringo ominously. The smell was getting so overpowering now, the boys were finding it hard to breathe. As they edged towards the front door – where the paint was peeling off the woodwork in ribbons – the air itself became thick and grey. Hand over his mouth and nose, Ringo reached forward and pressed the giant round doorbell. It made a sad, lonely clanging noise, as though it wasn't used very often. To the boys' surprise, the door opened a crack and fingers of yellowish-grey smoke curled through the narrow gap.

'Yes?' said an unpleasant voice that was somehow familiar.

'Trick or treat?' croaked Ringo, almost unable to speak.

'*Trick!*' cried the voice, throwing the door wide open. For a fleeting second the boys saw a man wearing an old-fashioned gas mask standing in the doorway. Another second, and great clouds of stinky yellow and grey smoke rolled out through the open door and the man vanished from view.

'*Run!*' Ringo yelled. His gang didn't need telling twice – they had already turned tail and were rushing back through the thick smog. Panting and wheezing, they staggered down the drive, through the gates and onto the pavement. They ripped off their Halloween masks so they could breathe better after choking on the foul air. But Ringo wasn't with them – he had tripped over in the drive and fallen onto the gravel. He was struggling to his feet when he saw the man from the big house walking towards him.

'*Help! Help!*' he yelled. The other members of his

gang stopped and turned, but no one wanted to go back for him. 'Quick!' said Zit, who was the smallest. 'Go and save Ringo!'

The other two just shuffled awkwardly and mumbled.

The spooky man wasn't wearing a gas mask any more and the boys could almost make out his features through the clearing smoke. Ringo was standing up now and the man seemed to be speaking to him, although the other boys couldn't hear what he said.

After a few minutes Ringo turned and waved to his gang. 'Oi!' he shouted. 'You lot! Get over here!'

Reluctantly the other three straggled towards him. Strangely, Ringo seemed very pleased with himself. Standing next to him, looking tweedy and just a tiny bit sinister, was none other than Dr Reeper.

Chapter Seventeen

'Good afternoon, boys,' said the teacher. He looked at them, standing there in their Halloween outfits, clutching their masks. 'How kind of you to think of including your poor old teacher in your jolly Halloween games.'

'But we didn't know . . .' protested Zit. The other two looked too surprised to speak. 'We wouldn't have, not if we'd known this was a *teacher's* house.'

'Don't you worry!' said Dr Reeper with a rather forced chuckle. 'I like to see young people enjoying themselves.' He waved a hand around to clear a bit of the lingering smelly smoke. 'I'm afraid you interrupted me just as I was in the middle of something. That's why it's a bit foggy round here.'

'Ugh! Were you cooking?' said Whippet unhappily. 'It stinks here.'

'No, not cooking – well, not food anyway,' said Dr Reeper. 'I was doing an experiment – I should get back to it. And I mustn't keep you here – I'm sure you have other people in the neighbourhood to delight with your amusing tricks.'

'What about . . . ?' said Ringo, trailing off deliberately before he reached the end of the sentence.

'Ah yes!' said Dr Reeper. 'Why don't you boys come and wait on the doorstep while I fetch something. I won't be a moment.'

The boys followed him as far as the open front door, where they hovered while Dr Reeper went in.

'What's going on?' Whippet hissed to Ringo as they waited.

'Right, gang,' said Ringo importantly. 'Gather round. Greeper wants us to do something for him. And he's gonna pay us.'

'Yeah, but what does he want us to do?' asked Tank.

'Relax, chill,' replied Ringo. 'It's nothing. He just wants us to deliver a letter – to the house with the weirdo in the spacesuit.'

'And he'll pay us for that?' squeaked Zit. 'Why?'

'I dunno,' admitted Ringo. 'And I don't really care. It's money, isn't it? That's what matters.' They waited for a bit longer. The minutes ticked by and yet there was still no sign of Greeper. Ringo peeked through the front door. 'Let's go in,' he said.

'We can't do that!' exclaimed the others.

'Yeah we can,' said Ringo, his eyes sparkling with mischief. 'Just think – at school we can tell everyone we've been inside Greeper's house! Let's see if we can nick something of his. Come on!' He tiptoed into the house, stopped and beckoned furiously for the others to follow. One by one they sidled through the front door.

In the hallway they saw a corridor with several doors leading off it. Everything in the hall was covered in dust, as though no one had touched it for a hundred years.

'This way,' ordered Ringo, sniggering with glee. He set off down the corridor, stopping in front of one of

the doors. 'I wonder what the old doc keeps in here.' He pushed it open. 'Well, well, what's all this?' he said, a sly smile spreading across his face as he peered in. 'Seems like there's more to the doc than meets the eye.' The other boys crowded round him to see what lay in the room beyond, their eyes widening as they took in the strange scene before them.

'Wow!' said Zit. 'What's in there?'

But before anyone could answer, Dr Reeper had reappeared in the corridor behind them.

'I asked you,' he said in the scariest voice imaginable, 'to wait outside.'

'Sorry sir sorry sir,' said the boys quickly, whisking round to face him.

'Did I invite you into my house? I don't think so. Perhaps you could explain why you have behaved so very badly? Or I will be forced to give you extra detention at school for disobedience.'

'Sir, sir,' said Ringo very fast, 'we were waiting outside but we were so interested to know . . . the experiment you talked about earlier . . . we wanted to come in and see.'

'You were?' said Dr Reeper suspiciously.

'Oh yes, sir!' chorused the boys enthusiastically.

'I wasn't aware that any of you were interested in science,' said Dr Reeper, sounding a little happier.

'Oh, sir, we love science, we do!' Ringo assured him in fervent tones. 'Tank here wants to be a scientist. When he grows up.' Tank looked rather startled but then tried to compose his face into what he hoped was an intelligent expression.

'Really?' said Dr Reeper, perking up no end. 'But this is wonderful news! You must all come into my laboratory – I've been longing to show someone what I've been working on and you seem like the perfect boys. Come in, do. I can tell you all about it.'

'What've you let us in for now?' muttered Whippet to Ringo as they followed Dr Reeper into the room.

'Shut up,' Ringo replied out of the corner of his mouth. 'It was this or detention. So look keen, all right? I'll get us out as soon as I can.'

Chapter Eighteen

D r Reeper's laboratory was clearly divided into two parts. On one side a strange-looking chemistry experiment was in progress. Lots of glass balls were linked to others via glass tubes. One of the balls was connected to what looked like a miniature volcano. Most of the volcano fumes funnelled upwards into the glass ball, but from time to time little wisps of them leaked out. Gases poured from one glass ball to the next, eventually ending up in one large ball in the centre. There was a cloud inside this last ball, and now and then they saw sparks flying about.

'So who wants to go first with the questions?' asked Dr Reeper, thrilled to have an audience.

Ringo sighed. 'Sir, what's that?' he said, pointing at the large chemistry experiment.

'Aha!' said Dr Reeper, grinning and rubbing his hands. 'I'm sure you remember the lovely rotten-egg stink you smelled when entering the house. Well, do you know what it is?'

'Rotten eggs?' piped up Tank, feeling pleased he knew the answer.

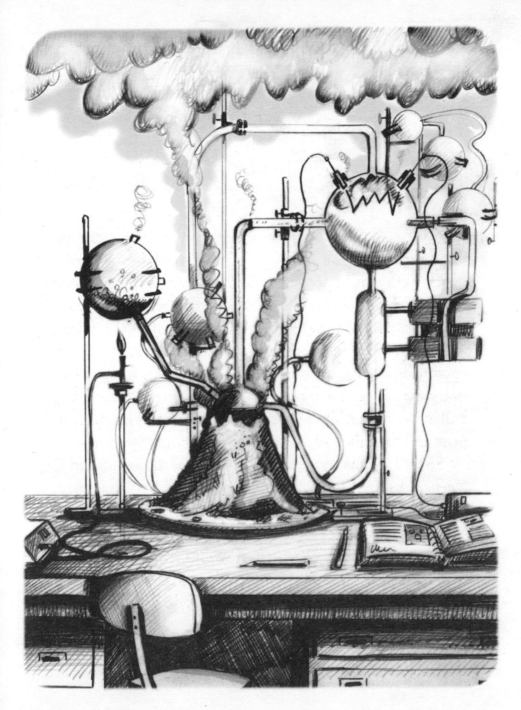

'Stupid child,' tutted Dr Reeper. 'You'll have to try harder than that if you want to become a scientist. Think! What could it be? Such an easy answer.'

The boys looked at each other and shrugged. 'Dunno,' they all murmured.

'Dear oh dear,' sighed Dr Reeper. 'Children today, they really do know nothing. It is the smell of the Earth – billions of years ago, when there was no life on it.'

'Well, how were we supposed to know that?' moaned Whippet.

But Dr Reeper took no notice of him. 'This isn't a real volcano obviously,' he continued, pointing at the small home-made volcano with smoke erupting from the crater at the top.

THE EARLY ATMOSPHERE

- The Earth's atmosphere hasn't always been as it is today. Were we to travel back 3.5 billion years (to when the Earth was about 1 billion years old), we would not be able to breathe.
- Today, our atmosphere is made of approximately 78% nitrogen, 21% oxygen and 0.93% argon. The remaining 0.07% is mostly carbon dioxide (0.04%) and a mixture of neon, helium, methane, krypton and hydrogen.
- The atmosphere 3.5 billion years ago contained no oxygen. It was mostly made of nitrogen, hydrogen, carbon dioxide and methane, but the exact composition is not known. What is known, however, is that huge volcanic eruptions occurred around that period, releasing steam, carbon dioxide, ammonia and hydrogen sulphide in the atmosphere. Hydrogen sulphide smells like rotten eggs and is poisonous when used in large amounts.

'Yeah, like, obviously,' murmured Ringo. 'I mean, like we hadn't noticed that.'

'It's just a little chemical reaction that emits the same kind of fumes,' Dr Reeper enthused, seemingly unaware of Ringo's rudeness. 'So I made it look like a little 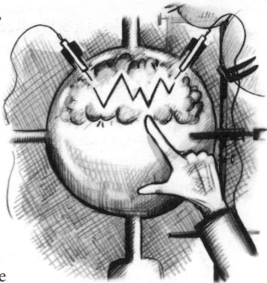 volcano with mud from the garden. I quite like it.'

The fumes from the volcano puffed upwards into a glass ball, where they mixed with water vapour. This came from another glass ball in which water was being heated over a gas burner. When they mixed together, the fumes and vapour formed a little cloud inside the large ball. Inside that cloud Dr Reeper had built a device that produced electrical sparks.

As the mini-volcano puffed dark smoke upwards, a little crackle of lightning shot across the cloud inside the ball. Dr Reeper tapped the glass gently.

'You see, when lightning strikes clouds of gas, strange reactions occur, and scientists have discovered that these reactions can sometimes lead to the formation of the most basic chemicals that life on Earth needs. These chemicals are called amino acids.'

MILLER & UREY'S EXPERIMENT

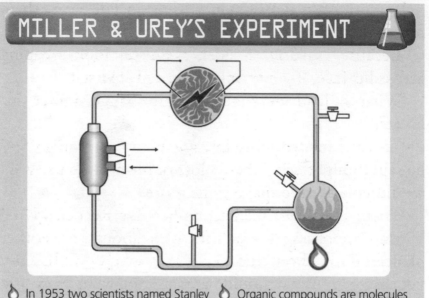

In 1953 two scientists named Stanley Miller and Harold Urey were working on the origin of life on Earth. They believed the ingredients for life could appear out of completely natural phenomena in the Earth's early atmosphere.

At that time (the 1950s) scientists had an idea about the kind of chemical compounds the early atmosphere probably contained. They also knew that lightning was frequent. So Miller and Urey conducted an experiment in which they stroked these chemical compounds with electric sparks (to mimic lightning). Astonishingly, they discovered that they had created special organic compounds.

Organic compounds are molecules that contain carbon and hydrogen. Some of these molecules, like the ones called amino acids, are necessary for life. Miller and Urey's experiment produced amino acids and gave hope to the scientific community that it may be possible to create life in a laboratory.

Today, however, more than fifty years after Miller and Urey, such a creation has yet to be achieved and we still do not know how life appeared on Earth. But we have been able to create, under special circumstances that mimic conditions on Earth a long time ago, more and more of the basic chemical building blocks of life.

'But why?' said Whippet. 'What do you want them for?'

'Because,' said Dr Reeper, a sinister look creeping across his face, 'I am trying to create Life itself.'

'What a load of rubbish,' said Ringo under his breath.

But Zit sounded more intrigued than his leader. 'Sir,' he said thoughtfully, 'there's lots of life around us. Why would you need to make some more?'

'There is on *this* planet,' replied Dr Reeper, giving him an approving look. 'But what about on another planet? What about another planet where life has not yet emerged? What would happen if we went there and took Life with us?'

'Sounds a bit stupid to me,' said Ringo. 'If we go to a new planet, there won't be anything there so there'll be nothing to do.'

'Oh, unimaginative boy!' cried Dr Reeper. 'We would be masters of the planet! It would be all ours.'

'But hang on a minute,' said Whippet, rather suspiciously. 'Where is this planet? An' how are we gonna get there?'

'All good questions,' said Dr Reeper. 'Come and have a look over here.'

He walked over to the other side of the room, which was covered with a huge picture of space and stars. In one corner there was a red circle around a couple of little white dots with lots of arrows pointing at it. Near the red circle was another circle drawn in green – except that the green circle seemed to be empty. Next to the map were white boards covered with diagrams and crazy-looking scribbles. There seemed to be some kind of link between the scribbles and the star poster.

Dr Reeper cleared his throat as the boys gathered around him. 'This, children, is the future!' he said, waving his hands towards the mad scribbles. '*Our* future! I expect,' he continued, 'you have never given a moment's thought to what I do when I'm not teaching you at school.'

The group nodded, agreeing that no, they hadn't.

'So let me save you the trouble. I' – Dr Reeper drew himself up to his full height so he towered over the

boys – 'am an expert on planets. I have worked all my life on planets, trying to find new ones.'

'D'you find any?' asked Whippet.

'I found many,' replied Dr Reeper proudly.

'But don't we know them all, like Mars or Saturn or Jupiter?' asked Whippet again.

The other boys nudged each other. 'Oo-er,' whispered Tank. 'Who'd have thought it? Whippet's a swot.'

'No, I'm not,' huffed Whippet crossly. 'It's just interesting, that's all.'

'Aha!' said Dr Reeper. 'You are right! We know all the planets that are around the star closest to the Earth, the star that we call the Sun. But I am looking for other ones! I am looking for planets that are around other stars, planets that are very far away. You see,' he continued, enjoying having his class – or a few of them anyway – actually listen to what he said for a change, 'a planet is not an easy thing to find. I have spent years collecting data from telescopes and I have looked at hundreds of planets in space. Unfortunately, most of the planets we have found so far are too close to their sun, making them too hot to support life and be habitable.'

'That's not gonna help then, is it?' said Whippet, sounding disappointed.

Dr Reeper pointed at his star map. 'But wait,' he said, 'I haven't told you everything yet. Out there in space are extraordinary, fantastic things, things that until now we have only been able to dream about. But the time is

EXOPLANETS

- An exoplanet is a planet that revolves around a star other than the Sun.
- So far, more than 240 exoplanets have been detected in space and new ones are discovered every month. This may not sound like a lot in comparison to the hundreds of billions of stars that are known to exist within the Milky Way alone, but this small number is mostly due to the difficulty of detecting them. A star is easy to detect because it is huge and emits light, whereas a planet is much smaller and only reflects the light of its star.
- Most of the techniques used to detect exoplanets are indirect, meaning that the exoplanet is not seen directly but the effects of its existence are. For instance, a big exoplanet will attract its star via gravity and will make the star move a bit. This star movement can be detected from Earth. 169 exoplanets have been found this

coming when all that will change, when man will go out across the cosmos and inhabit the whole Universe. Just imagine, boys, if we were the first to discover a whole new planet.'

'That's like that TV show,' said Zit cheerfully, 'where everyone gets on a spaceship and goes to a new planet where they get eaten by green aliens.'

'No, it's not like that at all!' snapped Dr Reeper. 'You must learn to distinguish between science fiction and science fact. This planet here that I have found' – his finger traced the red circle drawn in the corner of the map around the white dots – 'could be the new Planet Earth.'

'But it looks a bit of a long way to get to this here new planet,' said Whippet doubtfully.

'Yes, it is,' agreed the teacher. 'It is very, very, very far. So far away that if I had a phone conversation with way, and these are really big, much bigger than Jupiter, the largest of the Giant Planets of our Solar System.

- The *Corot* satellite launched in December 2006 is able to detect tiny changes in the amount of light shining from a star. Such changes can occur when an exoplanet (even a small one) passes in front of a star. The quality of the detectors *Corot* is equipped with should allow for the discovery of exoplanets much smaller than before, down to about twice the size of the Earth. We have not yet seen any Earth-sized exoplanets.

Only four exoplanets have been detected by direct imaging (i.e. by taking pictures) so far. These are also huge.

someone there, I would need to wait several years between the time I ask a question and the time they reply, just because of the time it would take my question to travel there and their reply to travel back again.'

'Did you talk with them on the phone?' the four kids said in unison.

'No, no, no!' tutted Dr Reeper in annoyance. 'I said *if* I had. Don't you understand anything?'

'But *is* there anyone out there?' Zit persisted, hopping from foot to foot in excitement.

'That's hard to tell,' said Dr Reeper. 'So I need to get out there and have a look.'

'How are you going do that?' queried Ringo, who despite himself was feeling interested now.

Dr Reeper gazed into the distance over their heads. 'I have been trying all my life to get into outer space,' he said. 'Once I nearly made it. But someone stopped me and I have never been able to forgive him. It was the greatest disappointment of my life. Ever since then, I've been looking for a way. And now I've got another chance. That's where you boys come in.' Dr Reeper reached for the letter in his pocket. 'Here is the letter that we spoke about in the driveway. Take it to George's friend. His name is Eric. Drop it in his letter box and make sure no one sees you,' said the teacher as he handed the letter over to Ringo.

'What's in it?' asked Ringo.

'Some information,' replied Dr Reeper. 'Information is power, boys. Always remember that.' Facing his star map and pointing with his burned hands towards the red

circle drawn around the bright dots, he said, 'And the information contained in this letter is the space location of this amazing new planet Earth number two.'

Whippet opcned his mouth to speak but Dr Reeper interrupted him.

'Drop off the letter *tonight*,' he said, cutting short any questions. 'And now it's time for you to go,' he added, hurrying them back out into the corridor.

'What about the cash?' asked Ringo sharply. 'When do we get our money?'

'Come and see me on Monday at school,' said Dr Reeper. 'If you've delivered the letter, I shall pay you handsomely. Now go.'

Chapter Nineteen

At lunch time on Monday George was sitting quietly in the school dining hall, minding his own business. He got out his lunchbox and looked inside it, wishing he could have bags of brightly coloured crisps or chocolate bars or fizzy orange like the other kids. Instead, he had a spinach sandwich, a hard-boiled egg, yet more broccoli muffins and some apple juice pressed by his mother. He took a large bite of his sandwich and sighed. He wished his parents would understand that he wanted to save the planet as much as they did but he wanted to do it in his own way. It was all very well for his parents to lead their alternative lifestyles because they only hung around with their friends, who were just like them.

They didn't have to go to school every day with people like Ringo and his gang laughing at them because they wore funny clothes and ate different food and didn't know what happened yesterday on the television. He tried to explain this to his dad but all he heard back was: 'We all have to do our bit, George, if we're going to save the Earth.'

George knew this was true; he just thought it was unfair and rather pointless that his *bit* meant him being a figure of fun at school and not having a computer at home. He had tried to explain to his parents how useful a computer could be.

'But, Dad,' he had pointed out, 'there's stuff you could do on a computer too, stuff that would help you with your work. I mean, you could get lots of information from the internet and organize your marches with email. I could set it all up for you and show you how.' George had gazed hopefully at his dad. He thought he saw a spark of interest in his dad's eyes but it flickered and died.

'I don't want to talk about it any more,' his dad had said. 'We're not getting a computer and that's final.'

That, thought George as he tried to swallow his lump of spinach sandwich, was why he had liked Eric so much. Eric had listened to George's questions and given him proper replies – ones that made sense to George. George wondered if he dared go round and see Eric later that afternoon. There was so much he wanted to ask him, and also he really wanted Eric to check his talk for the competition.

Just before lunch he had finally summoned up the courage to sign up on the board for the science competition, the one with a computer as the first prize. Under 'Topic' he had written: *My Amazing Rock from Outer Space*. It looked great as a title, although George still wasn't sure his talk was any good. He'd taken his lucky rock from outer space out of his pocket while he stood in front of the notice board, but to his horror had found it was crumbling into dust! It was his lucky charm – the little piece of the Solar System he had picked up near Saturn. The competition was the next day as well – George had only been allowed to enter at the last

minute because not enough kids from his school had signed up. The headteacher had been delighted to see George writing his name on the board.

He had bounced up as George filled out the form. 'Jolly good stuff, George! That's the spirit! We'll show them, won't we?' He beamed at George. 'We can't just let Manor Park walk away with every trophy in the area, can we now?' Manor Park was the local posh school which hogged all the prizes and won all the sports matches with boring regularity.

'Yes, sir,' said George, trying to stuff his outer space rock back into his pocket. But the sharp-eyed head spotted it.

'Oh dear, a handful of dirt,' he said, grabbing a nearby waste-paper bin. 'Chuck it in here, George. We can't have you going off to lunch with a pocket full of dust.' When George just stood there, rooted to the spot, the head rattled the bin impatiently under his nose. 'I was just the same as a boy,' he said, a claim George doubted. As far as he was concerned, the head had never been a boy; he'd been born wearing a suit and making enthusiastic comments about the Under-12 Football League. 'Pockets full of nonsense. Pop it in and off you go.'

Reluctantly George dropped the grey, crumbly remains of his most treasured possession into the bin. He promised himself he would come back later and try and save it.

As George munched his way through his sandwich, he thought about Eric and outer space and the competition the next day. While he was thinking, a hand crept over his shoulder and snatched a biscuit out of his lunchbox.

'Yum!' said Ringo's voice behind him. 'Ooh look, Georgie's famous muffins!' There was a squelching noise as Ringo took a large bite, followed by a spluttering sound as he spat it straight out again.

George didn't need to look round to know that the whole dining room would be staring in his direction and sniggering.

'Ugh, that's gross,' said Ringo, making fake gagging sounds behind him. 'Let's see if the rest is just as horrible.' His hand made another dive for George's lunch but George had had enough. As Ringo's big paw rootled inside the hand-made wooden box in which he kept his sandwiches, George slammed the lid down on his fingers.

'*Ow!*' squealed Ringo. 'Ow! Ow! Ow!' George opened the box again, allowing Ringo to pull out his hand.

'What's all this noise?' said the teacher on dinner duty, striding over. 'Can't you boys manage to do anything without causing trouble?'

'Sir, Doctor Reeper, sir!' screeched Ringo, who was cradling his damaged hand. 'I was just asking George what he had for lunch when he attacked me, sir, he did! You better give him double detention, sir, for the rest of term! He's broken my hand, sir!' Ringo smirked at Dr Reeper, who gave him a cool glance.

'Very well, Richard,' he said. 'Go and see the school nurse and come to my room when she's looked at your hand. I'll deal with George.' He ordered him away with a point of his finger, and Ringo slouched away, grinning to himself.

The rest of the dining room had fallen silent while they waited for Dr Reeper to announce George's

punishment. But Dr Reeper surprised them. Instead of giving George an earful, he just sat down next to him on the long bench. 'Carry on!' He waved a red hand at the rest of the room. 'Get on with your lunches. The bell will go soon enough, you know.' After a couple of seconds the usual hubbub started up again as everyone lost interest in George and went back to their conversations.

'So, George . . .' said Dr Reeper chummily.

'Yes, Doctor Reeper?' asked George nervously.

'How *are* you?' Dr Reeper sounded as though he really wanted to know.

'Oh, um, fine,' said George, rather taken aback.

'How are things at home?'

'They're . . . well . . . OK,' said George cautiously, hoping Greeper wasn't going to ask him about Cosmos.

'And how about your neighbour?' said Dr Reeper, trying and failing to sound casual. 'Have you seen him lately? Is he around at the moment? Or perhaps he has gone away . . .'

George tried to work out what answer Dr Reeper wanted so he could give him the opposite one.

'Perhaps people in the street are wondering where he's got to,' went on Dr Reeper, sounding spookier and spookier. 'Maybe it seems that he has just disappeared! Vanished from view! No idea where he might be! Is that it?' He peered hopefully at George, who was now convinced that there was something very wrong with Dr Reeper. 'Almost as though' – Dr Reeper sketched a shape in the air with his hands – 'he just flew off into outer space and never came back. Hmm? What about that, George? Is that what's happened, would you say?' The teacher was gazing at George, obviously wanting to hear that Eric had somehow melted away into thin air.

'Actually,' said George, 'I saw him this morning.' He hadn't but it seemed very important to tell Dr Reeper he had.

'Drat,' muttered Dr Reeper crossly, suddenly getting to his feet. 'Wretched boys.' He walked off without even bothering to say goodbye.

George closed up his lunchbox and decided to head back to the notice board so that he could look for his rock in the bin. As he hurried down the corridor, he passed Dr Reeper's study. He heard raised voices and stopped to listen through the door for a second.

'I told you to deliver the note!' rasped the familiar voice of Dr G Reeper.

'We did, didn't we?' whined a boy's voice, which sounded all too like Ringo's.

'You can't have done,' insisted Dr Reeper. 'You just can't have done.'

George would have stayed to listen for longer, but then the bell for lessons went and he desperately wanted to find his special outer-space rock before afternoon school began. However, when he got back to the bin, it had been emptied. There was only a clean plastic liner inside it. Saturn's mini-moon had gone.

Chapter Twenty

It was pouring with rain when George walked home that afternoon. Cold splats of water hurtled down from the dark grey sky as he trudged along. Cars dived through the big puddles at the edge of the road, sending tidal waves of dirty water swooshing over the pavement. By the time George reached his own street, he was shivering with cold. He got as far as Eric's door and hovered anxiously on the doorstep. He was longing to ring the bell and ask the scientist to help him with his talk for the next day. And he also wanted to find out why

Dr Reeper might think he had disappeared. But he was worried Eric would still be cross with him and send him away. To ring or not to ring? What to do? The skies were getting darker and darker, and suddenly he heard a huge clap of thunder. The rain got even heavier and George made up his mind. It was important to ask Eric about his talk and tell him about Dr Reeper. He decided to be brave and ring the bell.

Bing-bong! He waited for a few seconds and nothing happened. Just as he was wondering whether to ring again, the door flew open and Eric's head popped out.

'George!' he said in delight. 'It's you! Come in!' He reached out a long arm and whisked George inside, shutting the front door with a brisk slam. To his great surprise, George found himself standing in Eric's hallway, his wet coat dripping onto the bare floorboards.

'I'm so sorry,' he stammered.

'What for?' said Eric, looking a bit startled. 'What have you done?'

'About Annie . . . and the comet . . . and Cosmos,' George reminded him.

'Oh, that!' said Eric. 'I'd forgotten all about it! But now that you mention it, don't worry. Annie told me that it was her idea, not yours, and that she made you go into outer space. I take it that's true?' He looked at George over his heavy glasses, his bright eyes twinkling.

'Er, yes, actually, it is,' said George with relief.

'So really,' continued Eric, 'I should be saying sorry to *you*, for jumping to the wrong conclusion. Instead of considering all the evidence, I just applied some common sense – otherwise known as prejudice – and came up with totally the wrong answer.'

George didn't really understand all of this so he just nodded. From the library he could hear the sound of voices.

'Are you having a party?' he asked.

'Well, yes, a sort of party,' said Eric. 'It's a party of scientists so we like to call it a conference. Why don't you come in and listen? You might be interested. We're talking about Mars. Annie's had to miss it, I'm afraid, as she's still at her granny's. You can tell her about it if you stay.'

'Oh, yes please!' said George, forgetting in his excitement to ask about his talk or tell Eric about Dr Reeper. As he took off his wet coat and followed Eric into the library, he could hear a woman's voice.

'... this is the reason why my colleagues and I strongly advocate a thorough search of our closest neighbour. Who knows, in the end, what we may find by digging underneath the red surface ...'

Eric and George tiptoed into the library. It looked quite different from the last time George had seen it. All the books were neatly arranged on shelves, pictures of the Universe hung on the wall in frames, and in the corner lay a pile of carefully folded spacesuits. In the middle of the room, on rows of chairs, sat a group of scientists who were all different shapes and sizes and looked like they came from all over the world. Eric showed George to a seat, a finger pressed to his lips to show that George should keep very quiet.

Standing at the front of the room was the speaker, a tall, beautiful woman with a plait of thick red hair so long it reached right down past her waist. Her green eyes glittered as she smiled at the scientists gathered for

the conference. Just above her head, Cosmos's window portal was showing a red planet. The red-haired speaker continued her talk.

'Isn't it highly probable that evidence of life, had life existed on Mars in long-gone times, is not there for us to find on the surface? We should never forget that every now and then, sandstorms radically alter the planet's surface, burying deeper and deeper beneath layers of inorganic dust the entire past of our red neighbour.'

As she spoke, they all saw through Cosmos's window an enormous sandstorm that took over the whole surface of the red planet.

Eric bent his head towards George and whispered, 'What she means is that even if there was once life on

Mars, we wouldn't see it on the surface today. In fact, I can tell you, this scientist strongly believes there was life on Mars at some stage. She sometimes even declares that there still *is* life there. That would be one of the most amazing discoveries of all time. But we can't say much more than that at this stage. We need to get onto this beautiful red planet ourselves to find out.'

George was about to ask why Mars was red, but realized that the speaker was finishing her talk.

'Do you have any questions before we have a short break?' she asked her audience. 'After tea and biscuits we will discuss our last and most important issue.'

George felt very sad that he had only heard the end of the talk, so he raised his hand to ask something.

Meanwhile all the scientists were murmuring, 'Ooh, tea!' None of them wanted to ask a question.

'So let's have our well-deserved tea break then,' said Eric, who hadn't spotted George's raised hand.

The scientists rushed over to the tea table in the corner of the room, anxious to nab all the Jammy Dodgers before the others could scoff them.

But the red-haired speaker had noticed George's thin arm waving in the air. 'Well, well,' she said, looking at George. 'Colleagues, we do have a question after all and it's from our new fellow down here.'

The other scientists turned and looked at George. When they saw how small he was, they all smiled and brought their cups of tea and biscuits back to their seats.

'What would you like to know?' asked the speaker.

'Er . . . Please . . . If you don't mind,' said George, suddenly feeling very shy. He wondered if his question was a really stupid one and whether everyone would laugh at him. He took a deep breath. 'Why is Mars red?' he asked.

'Good question!' said one of the other scientists, blowing on his tea. George breathed a sigh of relief. Professor

Crzkzak, the red-haired speaker, whose name no one ever managed to pronounce, nodded and started to give George an answer.

'If you walk through the hills and mountains here on Earth, you can sometimes see red patches of ground that are not covered with any plants. This is true, for instance, in the Grand Canyon in the United States. But there are many other places where this is also the case. The ground is this red colour because there is iron there that has rusted. When iron becomes oxidized – which is another way of saying that it has rusted – it becomes red. It is because of the presence of oxidized iron, I mean rusted iron, that the surface of Mars is red.'

'Do you mean that Mars is made of iron?' asked George.

'Well, not quite. Since we sent some robots to Mars, we know that it is just a thin layer of rusted iron powder that gives Mars its red colour. It seems that underneath the layer of red dust, the surface of Mars may be quite similar to the surface of the Earth – without the water, that is.'

'So there is no water on Mars?'

'There is, but the water we know of is not liquid. On Mars it's far too hot during the day – any water turns into vapour and is lost. So the only places where water can remain are those where the temperature always

MARS

Mars is the fourth closest planet to the Sun.

Average distance to the Sun: 141.6 million miles (227.9 million km)
Diameter at equator: 4,228.4 miles (6,805 km)
Surface area: 0.284 x Earth's surface area
Volume: 0.151 x Earth's volume
Mass: 0.107 x Earth's mass
Gravity at the equator: 37.6% of Earth's gravity at Earth's equator

Mars is a rocky planet with an iron core. In between its core and its red crust there is a thick rocky layer. Mars also has a very thin atmosphere mostly made of carbon dioxide (95.3%) which we cannot breathe. The average temperature on Mars is very cold: around -60°C (-76°F).

**The largest volcanoes in the Solar System
are on the surface of Mars.**

The largest one of all is called Olympus Mons. From one side to the other, it spreads over a disc-shaped area 403 miles (648 km) wide and is 15 miles (24 km) high. On Earth the largest volcano is on Hawaii. It is called Mauna Loa and reaches 2.54 miles (4.1 km) in height from sea level – though if one measures it from where its base starts at the bottom of the ocean, it rises 10.5 miles (17 km) high.

remains cold, day and night, so that water can freeze and remain frozen. This happens at the poles. At the north pole of Mars we have found large quantities of frozen water: ice. It is the same on Earth, where large ice reservoirs can be found at the poles, in the Arctic and the Antarctic. Does that answer your question?'

Since Mars has an atmosphere, one can talk about Martian weather. It very much resembles what the weather would be like on a very cold desert-covered Earth. Sandstorms are common and huge cyclonic storms of water-ice clouds measuring more than ten times the size of the United Kingdom have been observed.

○ Mars is believed to have once been at the right temperature for liquid water to flow on its surface and carve the channels we can now see on its surface. Today, the only confirmed water presence there is in the ice caps at the poles, where ice-water is mixed with solid carbon dioxide.

○ In December 2006, however, scientists looking at pictures of newly formed gullies on the Martian surface suggested a striking possibility: liquid water may still be present on Mars, buried deep down under its surface.

Mars has two small moons: Phobos and Deimos.

'Yes, thank you!' said George. He was just busy thinking up another question when Eric stood up at the front of the room, next to the speaker.

'Thank you, Professor Crzkzak,' he said, 'for your very interesting paper on Mars.'

Professor Crzkzak bowed and went to take her seat.

'Dear friends and colleagues,' continued Eric. 'Before we move on to the last and most important issue we have to discuss, let me thank you all for making the effort to get here. Some of you have come from far across the globe but I know the talks we have heard today have made the journey worthwhile. I'm sure I need hardly remind you how important it is that the existence of Cosmos stays a closely guarded secret.'

The group nodded their agreement.

'Now,' continued Eric, 'the question we all came to answer is a question of fundamental interest for everyone who is involved in science. We all know far too well how it can be used for evil purposes, and that is why we have all taken the Oath of the Scientist, so that science is used only for the good of humanity. But we are now facing a dilemma. As you heard in the news and saw at the eco march on Saturday, more and more people are concerned about the state of the Earth. So, the question we now have to answer is: Should we concentrate on finding ways to improve life on Earth and face its problems, or should we try to find another planet for humanity to inhabit?'

All the scientists in the room were silent and looked very serious. George watched them as they wrote an answer on a little piece of paper. Eric then collected the papers into a hat. In total, including Eric and the red-haired speaker, eight scientists had voted. Eric then started to open up the papers one by one.

'The Earth.'

'The Earth.'

'Another planet.'

'Another planet.'

'Another planet.'

'The Earth.'

'The Earth.'

'Another planet.'

'Well, well,' said Eric. 'It seems we have a split vote.'

The red-haired Professor Crzkzak put her hand up. 'May I make a suggestion?' she asked. Everyone else nodded. She got to her feet. 'George,' she said, addressing the boy directly, 'we may lack a bit of perspective on this matter, because we are all specialists in our fields. So you could maybe tell us what you think about it.'

All the scientists were looking at him now. George felt very shy, and stayed silent for a few seconds.

'Say what you really think,' whispered Professor Crzkzak.

Twisting his fingers in his lap, George thought about his parents and the green campaigners. He then thought about the excitement of travelling in space and trying to find another home out there. And then he heard himself say to the scientists:

'Why can't you do both?'

Chapter Twenty-One

'George, you are absolutely spot on,' Eric said as they waved goodbye to all the scientists, who were leaving now that the conference had come to an end. George and Eric went back into the library, which was covered in biscuit wrappers, half-drunk cups of tea, old biros and conference papers folded into aeroplane shapes. 'We need to work on saving this planet *and* looking for a new one. We don't have to do one or the other.'

'Do you think you will?' asked George. 'You and your friends? Do both, I mean?'

'Oh, I think so, yes,' said Eric. 'Maybe we could invite your parents to our next conference? Do you know, George, I heard your father's talk at the climate-change protest march the other day. Maybe he has some good ideas we could use?'

'Oh no, don't do that!' said George, panicking. He wasn't at all sure that his father would approve of Eric and his friendly scientists. 'I don't think he'd like that.'

'He might surprise you,' said Eric. 'We all need to

work together to save the planet if we're to get anything done.' He started to clear up some of the mess the scientists had made. They seemed to have left behind an extraordinary number of things: jackets, hats, jumpers – even a shoe.

'It was very nice of you to drop by to apologize,' said Eric, gathering together a great armful of abandoned clothing.

'Well, actually,' admitted George, 'that's not quite why I came round.' Eric dumped the clothes in a corner of the room and turned back to look at him. 'I signed up for a science competition,' the boy continued nervously.

'It's a bit like your conference, except it's kids giving the talks. And there's a big computer as first prize. I've tried to write something to say but I'm really worried I've made loads of mistakes and everyone will laugh at me.'

'Yes, Annie told me about your competition,' said Eric, looking serious. 'And I've got something that might help you. Funnily enough, I had an idea after your comet ride. I decided to start writing a book about the Universe for you and Annie – I've made some notes. They might help you with your science presentation.' He picked up a plate of biscuits. 'Have one of these. Brain food.'

George helped himself to what was left of the biscuits.

'How about this for an idea?' said Eric thoughtfully. 'If you could just give me a hand to get my library tidied up a bit – Annie's left me strict instructions that I'm not to make the house messy while she's away – then we can talk about your science presentation and I'll go through the notes I made for you. Does that sound like a fair deal?'

'Oh yes!' said George, delighted by Eric's promise. 'What would you like me to do?'

'Oh, perhaps a bit of sweeping or something like that,' said Eric vaguely. He leaned casually on a wobbly pile of chairs as he spoke, accidentally pushing them over with a loud crash.

George burst out laughing.

'You can see why I need help,' said Eric apologetically but his eyes were twinkling with laughter. 'I'll pick up these chairs and maybe you could brush a bit of this mud off the floor? Would you mind?'

The carpet was covered in footprints left by the scientists, none of whom ever remembered to wipe their feet on the doormat.

'Not at all,' said George, stuffing the last biscuit into his mouth and running off to the kitchen, where he found a dustpan and brush. He came back into the library and started to swish away at some of the worst bits of dirt. As he worked, a piece of paper stuck to his brush. He picked it off the bristles and was about to throw it away when he realized it was a letter, addressed to *Eric*. There was something strangely familiar about the handwriting.

'Look at this!' He passed the note to Eric. 'Someone must have dropped it.' Eric took the piece of paper and unfolded it while George carried on sweeping. Suddenly he heard a great shout.

'Eureka!' cried Eric. George looked up. Eric was just standing there, piece of paper in hand, a joyous look on his face.

'What's going on?' George asked him.

'I've just been given the most amazing piece of information!' cried Eric. 'If this is correct . . .' He peered at the piece of paper again, holding it up very close to his thick glasses. He muttered a long string of numbers to himself.

'What is it?' asked George.

'Hang on.' Eric seemed to be calculating something in his head. He ticked off a series of points on his fingers, screwed up his face and scratched his head. 'Yes!' he said. 'Yes!' He stuffed the paper in his pocket, then picked George up off his feet and whirled him around. 'George, I've got the answer! I think I know!' Suddenly dropping him again, Eric went over to Cosmos and started typing.

'What do you know?' said George, who was a little dizzy.

'Great Shooting Stars! This is brilliant.' Eric was frantically tapping on the computer's keyboard. A huge flash of light shot out of Cosmos's screen into the middle of the room and George saw that the great computer was once more making a doorway.

'Where are you going?' George asked. Eric was struggling into a spacesuit but he was in such a hurry that he put both feet into one trouser leg and fell over. George hauled him up again and helped him on with the suit.

'So *exciting*!' said Eric as he buckled it up.

'What is?' said George, who was now feeling rather alarmed.

'The letter, George. The letter. This might be it! This might be what we've all been looking for.'

'Who was the letter from?' asked George, who had a bad feeling inside his stomach, although he didn't know why.

'I'm not sure,' admitted Eric. 'It doesn't really say.'

'Then you shouldn't trust it!' said George.

'Oh rubbish, George,' said Eric. 'I expect it was written by someone at the conference who wanted me to check out the information using Cosmos. I expect they wanted to know it was correct before they announced it to the whole scientific community.'

'Then why didn't they just ask you directly? Why write a letter?' persisted George.

'Because because because,' said Eric, sounding a little annoyed. 'They probably had a good reason which I'll find out when I get back from my trip.'

George saw that Cosmos's screen was now covered in long strings of numbers. 'What are those?' he asked.

'That's the co-ordinates of my new journey,' said Eric.

'Are you going now?' asked George sadly. 'What about my science presentation?'

Eric stopped in his tracks. 'Oh, George, I am

sorry!' he exclaimed. 'But I really have to go, it's too important to wait Your talk will be fine without me! You'll see . . .'

'But—'

'No *buts*, George,' said Eric, putting on his glass space helmet and speaking in his funny space voice once more. 'Thank you so much for finding that letter! It has given me a vital clue. Now I must go. G-o-o-o-d-b-y-e-e-e-e!'

Eric leaped through the portal doorway and was gone into outer space before George had time to say another word. The portal slammed shut behind him, and George was left alone in the library.

Chapter Twenty-Two

After the door to outer space closed, there was a moment of deathly silence in the library. It was broken by the sound of a tune playing very faintly in the background. George looked around to see who might be humming but then he realized it was Cosmos, singing a little song to himself as he crunched the long strings of numbers that were flashing across his screen.

'*Ba-ba-ba-ba,*' tooted Cosmos.

'Cosmos,' said George, who wasn't feeling very happy about Eric's sudden departure. He certainly didn't feel like whistling a merry tune.

'*Tum-ti-tum-tum,*' said Cosmos in reply.

'Cosmos,' repeated George, 'where has Eric gone?'

'*Tra-la-la-la,*' Cosmos carried on cheerfully, rolling reams of endless numbers across his screen.

'Cosmos!' said George once more, this time with more urgency. 'Stop singing! *Where has Eric gone?*'

The computer stopped mid-hum. 'He has gone to find a new planet,' he said, sounding rather surprised. 'I'm sorry you don't like my music,' he continued. 'I

was just singing while I worked. *Pom-pom-pom-pom*,' he started again.

'*Cosmos!*' yelled George. '*Where is he?*'

'Well, that's hard to say,' replied Cosmos.

'How come you don't know?' said George, surprised. 'I thought you knew everything.'

'Unfortunately not. I don't know what I have not been shown.'

'Do you mean Eric is lost?'

'No, not lost. His travels uncover new places for me. I follow him and I map the Universe.'

'All right,' said George, relieved to know Eric wasn't lost. 'Fine. I suppose it must be something very special that he's gone to see, for him to rush off like that—'

'No, no,' interrupted Cosmos. 'Just another undiscovered part of the Universe. All in a day's work.'

George felt a bit confused. If that was the case, why had Eric just shot off into outer space in such a tearing hurry? He'd thought that Eric was his friend and that, unlike other adults, he would explain what he was up to and why. But he hadn't. He had just gone.

For a split second George wondered about grabbing a spacesuit, asking Cosmos to open the portal and joining Eric. But then he remembered how furious Eric had been after he and Annie had gone into outer space without his permission. He realized sadly that he would just have to go home now. Maybe Eric wasn't really his friend at all but just another grown-up who didn't think it mattered whether George understood stuff or not. He picked up his wet coat and school bag and made for the door; Cosmos was still humming his little melody in the background.

George opened Eric's front door to leave. He was just about to step out into the street when he had a sudden flash of memory. There had

been *two* reasons he had come to see Eric today and he'd only managed to tell him about one of them: the science competition. In all the excitement he'd quite forgotten to warn Eric about Dr Reeper and his strange questions.

The letter, George now remembered. It's Greeper! George had overheard him asking the bullies to deliver a note! *That must be the letter Eric received! And Reeper asked if Eric had disappeared!* George turned and rushed straight back into the house, leaving the door wide open behind him.

In the library, Cosmos was still at work. On the desk in front of him, George spotted the letter that Eric had read with such joy. He read it through, his hands shaking as he realized who had written it.

Dear Eric,

I understand that your longstanding quest to find new planets to inhabit isn't yet over.

I wanted to draw your attention to a very particular planet I happen to have found. It is roughly the size of the Earth and lies at about the same distance from its star as the Earth is from the Sun. As far as I know, there has never been such a strong candidate planet for humans to settle on. I am pretty sure it has an atmosphere like ours. An atmosphere we could breathe.

I'm not in a position to verify this information, but I very much look forward to hearing what you think of it. Please see below for the co-ordinates of that planet, or rather, a way to reach it.

Scientifically yours,

G.R.

George knew perfectly well who 'G.R.' was. The handwriting was all too familiar to him – he recognized it from his school reports, which usually said things like, *George will amount to nothing unless he learns to pay attention in class and stop daydreaming.* It was without doubt written by Dr Reeper.

And Greeper knows Cosmos exists! It must be a trap! George thought. 'Cosmos!' he said out loud, interrupting the computer, who was now humming 'Twinkle Twinkle Little Star'. 'You have to take me to Eric right now! Can you find him?'

'I can try,' replied Cosmos. A succession of images appeared on his screen. The first one looked like a starfish, with long arms twisted into some sort of spiral. Above it was written: OUR GALAXY, THE MILKY WAY.

'Our galaxy, the Milky Way, is made of approximately two hundred billion stars,' Cosmos started. 'Our star, the Sun, is only one of them —'

Chapter Twenty-Three

'No!' howled George. 'Not another lecture! I haven't got time – this is an emergency, Cosmos.'

The picture of the Milky Way zoomed inside the spiral very quickly, as if Cosmos was offended by George's lack of interest. George could see that the spiral was indeed made of countless stars. The image whizzed past these until it reached a place where there didn't seem to be anything any more. The picture stopped moving. The screen looked as if it had been cut in two. The bottom half of the screen was full of stars, the other half completely empty except for a thin line that was moving up towards the top edge of the screen. The empty part of the screen seemed to correspond to an unknown part of the Universe – an unknown part which the thin line seemed to be unravelling as it moved.

Pointing at the upper end of the line was a moving arrow with a little tag attached to it. The writing was so small, George could hardly read it.

'What does it say?' he asked Cosmos.

Cosmos didn't reply, but the tag grew bigger, and George saw the word ERIC written on it.

'There he is! Open the portal for me! Near that arrow,' commanded George, pressing the ENTER key on Cosmos's keyboard.

'George is a member of the Order. Authorization granted. Spacesuit needed,' Cosmos said in the mechanical voice he used to process orders.

George rummaged through the pile of spacesuits but he couldn't see the one he'd worn before. Eric's old spacesuits were all huge so he reluctantly ended up wearing Annie's old pink one. It was a bit tight and he felt very silly, but as the only person he was going to see in outer space was Eric, he figured it didn't matter. Once he was snugly buckled into the sequinned suit, Cosmos drew the doorway into outer space.

George reached forward and opened the door.

Holding onto the portal frame with his hands, he leaned out to have a look around, his feet still anchored inside Eric's library. This part of outer space seemed very similar to the one he had seen before, but this time he didn't see any planets around him. It didn't look much like the image on Cosmos's screen – it wasn't cut in two at all. There were stars shining everywhere. Eric, however, was nowhere to be seen.

'*Eric!*' George shouted. '*Eric! Can you hear me?*'

There was no reply.

Maybe he was in the wrong place.

George looked back into the library, towards Cosmos's screen; the ERIC arrow was still there. Next to it he saw a new one that had GEORGE written on it. He realized that what he saw out of the doorway wasn't yet on Cosmos's screen. Cosmos had to process the information and only after he had done so, would it appear on the screen.

George leaned through the door into outer space once more, making sure not to fall. '*Eric! Are you there? Can you hear me?*' he yelled.

'Who's calling me?' replied a faint voice through the transmitter fitted inside George's space helmet.

'*Eric! Where are you? Do you see the door?*'

'Oh, hello! George! Yes, I can see you. Stop shouting now, you're hurting my ears. I'm coming straight towards you from your left.'

George looked to his left and there it was, a little asteroid, gently travelling through space. Sitting on it

was Eric, holding in each hand a rope attached to spikes he had planted in the rock. He looked very relaxed.

'What are you doing?' he asked.

'Come back!' cried George, trying to sound urgent without shouting. 'It's Greeper who sent you the letter! It's my fault! I spoke to him about Cosmos!'

'George,' replied Eric firmly, 'right now I'm working, so we'll have to talk about this later. You definitely shouldn't have mentioned Cosmos to anyone. Close the portal, George, and go home!'

'You don't understand!' said George. 'Greeper is horrible! I know him, he's my teacher! It must be a trap! Come back now! Please! This morning he asked me if you had disappeared!'

'That's enough! And stop being silly! Look around – there's nothing dangerous at all,' said Eric impatiently. 'Now go home and forget about Cosmos. I'm not sure I should have shown you my computer after all.'

George looked over at Eric's rock. In a few seconds it was going to be close enough for him to jump onto it. He took a few steps back into the library, paused for a second and then ran towards the doorway, leaping through it as far towards the rock as he could.

'Holy planet!' he heard Eric say. '*George! Grab my hand!*'

Chapter Twenty-Four

As George flew through space, he just managed to hold onto Eric's hand. Eric hauled him onto the rock, sitting him down beside him. Behind them, the doorway back into Eric's library vanished.

'*George, are you crazy?!* If I hadn't caught your hand, you could have been lost in space for ever!' said Eric, sounding furious all over again.

'But—' said George.

'*Silence!* I'm sending you back! *Now!*'

'*No!*' shouted George. '*Listen to me! This is really important.*'

'What is?' said Eric, suddenly aware that there was something very wrong in George's voice. 'What is it, George?'

'*You have to*

come back with me!' babbled George. 'I'm really really sorry and it's all my fault but I told my teacher from school about Cosmos – I told Doctor Reeper and then he sent you the letter about the planet!' Before Eric could say anything George rushed on, 'And this morning he asked me if you'd disappeared! He did! It's true! It's a trick, Eric! He's out to get you!'

'Greeper . . . Reeper! . . . I see!' said Eric. 'So the letter is from Graham! He found me again.'

'Graham?' asked George, astonished.

'Yes, Graham Reeper,' Eric replied calmly. 'We used to call him Grim.'

'You *know* him?' George gasped with shock underneath his space helmet.

'Yes, I do. A long, long time ago we used to work together. But we had an argument which led to an awful accident. Reeper got very badly burned, and after that he went off on his own. We stopped him being a member of the Order in the end because we were so worried about what he might get up to. But do you know what he sent me in that letter?'

'Yeah,' said George, remembering how Eric left without saying goodbye. 'Just another planet.'

'*Just* another planet? George, you must be joking! The planet Graham told me about is one where humans could live! I've been looking for such a place for ages, and there it is!' Pointing towards two little dots in front of him – one big and bright, the other smaller and less bright – Eric added, '*It's right there!* The big bright dot there is a star, and the smaller dot is the planet we're heading for. It doesn't actually shine on its own – it just reflects the light of its star, like the Moon reflects the light of the Sun at night.'

'But Greeper is horrible!' objected George, who really couldn't understand why Eric and Cosmos always had to be in lecturing mode in times of danger. 'He would never have given you the co-ordinates of that planet just like that! There *must* be a trick.'

'Oh come on, George,' said Eric. 'You know that I can get Cosmos to open up the portal to take us home again any time I want. We're quite safe. It's true that your teacher and I had our differences in the past, but I expect he's decided to put it behind him and join in the efforts we're making to explore and understand the Universe. And I have installed new antennae on our helmets. We can now communicate with Cosmos even if they get damaged.'

'Why didn't you ask Cosmos to just send you there directly? Let's do just that – let's get back to your library.'

'Aha!' said Eric. 'We can't do that. Cosmos doesn't know what lies ahead of us, and that's my job – to go where computers cannot. After I've been somewhere new, then we can use Cosmos to go there again, like you just did to find me here. But the first trip I always need to do myself.'

'Are you sure it's safe?' asked George.

'Positive,' said Eric confidently.

George and Eric fell silent for a few moments, and George started to feel a bit better. He managed to stop thinking about Greeper and look around him to see where he was. In all his eagerness to warn Eric, he had quite forgotten he was on a rock in outer space!

To be fair to Eric, everything around them seemed calm. They could see clearly in all directions, and the star with its planet was growing bigger and bigger as their rock approached it.

But then something started to go wrong with the path of the rock. Just as George's comet had changed direction when it flew past the Giant Planets and the Earth, their rock seemed to be switching course. But this time there didn't seem to be any planets around them. The rock was now heading in a completely different direction, away from the distant planet Eric so much wanted to see.

'What's going on?' George asked Eric.

'I'm not sure!' replied Eric. 'Look around and let me know if you see any place in the sky where there is no star! And Cosmos, open the portal, just in case.'

Cosmos didn't seem to have heard Eric's request since no portal appeared nearby.

George and Eric looked in the direction the rock was heading. Everywhere, all around them, were stars – except for an area on their right, where there was a small patch of sky containing no stars, which was becoming larger and larger all the time.

'Over there!' George said to Eric, pointing towards the growing dark patch. The stars around it were moving in a very strange way, as if space itself were being distorted by it.

'*Oh, no!*' shouted Eric. '*Cosmos, open the portal now! Now!*'

But no portal appeared.

'*What is it?*' asked George, who was becoming scared.

The dark area now covered more than half the space

they were looking at, and all the stars they could see outside it were moving erratically, even though they were far behind it.

'*Cosmos!*' shouted Eric once more.

'T-r-y-i-n-g . . .' Cosmos replied in a very faint voice, but nothing happened.

George's mind was starting to spin! In front of them, the dark area was becoming enormous. All the space around George and Eric was warped, and some dark patches started to appear to their left and right. George could no longer tell up from down, or right from left. All he knew for sure was that the dark patch was getting bigger and bigger, from all sides, as if it wanted to eat them up.

'*Cosmos! Hurrrrreeee!*' Eric yelled.

A very faint doorway started to appear in front of them. Eric grabbed George by the belt of his spacesuit and threw him towards it. As he flew through, George saw Eric trying to reach it too. He was shouting something, but his voice was distorted and it was hard to make sense of it.

Just before landing on Eric's library floor, just before the portal door shut and the view of outer space disappeared, George saw the dark patch engulf Eric entirely. It was only then that he understood what Eric had been saying.

'*Find my new book!*' Eric had shouted. '*Find my book on black holes!*'

Jupiter is the largest planet in the Solar System. The black dot on the right is the shadow of one of Jupiter's moons. The Great Red Spot on the left is a storm that has been observed from Earth for over 300 years.

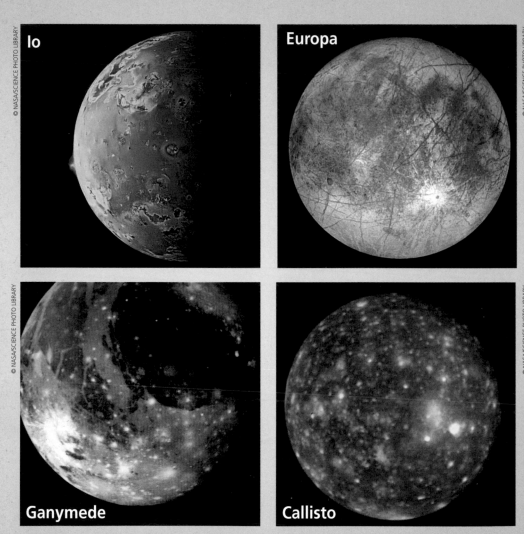

Io

Europa

Ganymede

Callisto

© NASA/SCIENCE PHOTO LIBRARY

The largest moons of Jupiter. Io is known to have intense volcanic activity. Europa is thought to hide an ocean of liquid water more than 60 miles (100 km) deep underneath an icy crust. There are ancient impact craters on Ganymede, and erosion processes have been detected on Callisto.

A Martian sunset seen by the Mars exploration rover *Spirit* on 19 May 2005.

Mars. The orange area in the centre is a large dust storm, and the bluish-white areas at the top and left are water-ice clouds.

Mars with its moons.

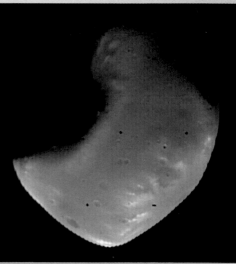

The Martian moons are too small to be round. And this is Deimos, the smallest and outermost.
This is Phobos, the largest and innermost.

This panorama of Mars is from the top of Husband Hill, a peak in the Columbia Hills, which are named in memory of the astronauts who died in the space shuttle *Columbia*. It was taken in August 2005 by the exploration rover *Spirit*.

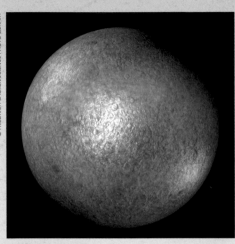

© FRIEDRICH SAURER/SCIENCE PHOTO LIBRARY

Computer artwork of the dwarf planet Ceres, the largest object in the asteroid belt. No spacecraft has yet reached any of the dwarf planets.

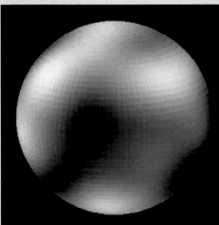

© NASA/ESA/STSCI/A.STERN,SWRI/SCIENCE PHOTO LIBRARY

Computer-processed image from the Hubble Space Telescope of the dwarf planet Pluto.

© FRIEDRICH SAURER/SCIENCE PHOTO LIBRARY

Computer artwork of the dwarf planet Eris. Eris is the largest and outermost of the three dwarf planets in the Solar System.

Chapter Twenty-Five

George fell back through the door and landed on the floor with a heavy *thump*. This time the journey back from outer space to Eric's library had seemed to suck all the breath out of him and he had to lie on the floor for a few seconds, panting, before he could get up. When he staggered to his feet, he hoped he would see Eric hurtling through the doorway behind him. But instead, all he saw was the outline of the door, which had become faint and wavy. It seemed to be fading into nothing. He yelled out, '*Eric!*' but got no reply. A millisecond later, the door vanished entirely.

'*Cosmos!*' shouted George, undoing his glass space helmet. 'Quick! Cosmos, we have to get—'

But as he turned round to face the great computer, he had his second great shock. Where Cosmos should have been, there was just a spaghetti tangle of coloured wires and an empty space. Looking wildly around the room, George saw that the library door was ajar. He ran through it and into the hallway, to find the front door wide open and the cold night air blowing in. With

no time to take off his spacesuit, he dashed into the street, where he could make out the shapes of four boys running along the road. One of them was carrying a bulky rucksack with a few wires sticking out of the top of it. George hurried after them as fast as he could in his heavy suit. As he stumbled along, familiar voices drifted back to him on the wind.

'Oi, careful with that!' George heard Ringo shout.

'Beep! Beep!' came a noise from the rucksack. 'Unlawful action! Unauthorized command!'

'When's it going to shut up?' shouted Tank, who was carrying the rucksack. 'How come it can speak when it isn't even plugged in?'

'Help! Help!' came the mechanical voice from the rucksack. 'I am being kidnapped! I am the world's most amazing computer! You cannot do this to me! Alarm! Alarm!'

'It'll run out of batteries soon,' said Whippet.

'Unhand me, you villains!' said the voice inside the rucksack. 'This bouncing around is bad for my circuits.'

'I'm not carrying it any further!' said Tank, coming to a sudden halt. George immediately stopped in his tracks.

'Someone else can take over,' he heard Tank say.

'All right,' said Ringo in a menacing voice. 'Give it here. Right, now, little computer. *You* will *shut up* for the rest of the journey or I will take you to pieces bit by bit until you are just a big pile of microchips.'

'Eek!' said the computer.

'D'you understand?' said Ringo in fierce tones.

'Of course I understand,' said the computer snootily. 'I am Cosmos, the world's most amazing computer. I am programmed to understand concepts so complex that your brain would explode if you were even to—'

'*I said*,' snarled Ringo, opening the top of the rucksack and speaking down into it, '*shut up!* Which bit of those two words don't you get, you moron?'

'I am a peaceful computer,' replied Cosmos in a small voice. 'I am not used to threats or violence.'

'Then be quiet,' replied Ringo, 'and we won't threaten you.'

'Where are you taking me?' whispered Cosmos.

'To your new home,' said Ringo, shouldering the rucksack. 'C'mon, gang, let's get there.' The boys set off at a run once more.

George staggered after them as fast as he could but he was unable to keep up. After a few more minutes he lost them in the foggy dark night. There was no point in running any further – he couldn't tell which way they had gone. But even so, he felt sure he knew who had asked Ringo and his friends to break in and steal Cosmos. And knowing that was the first step to finding the super computer again.

As Ringo and the boys ran off into the night, George turned and walked back to Eric's house, where the front door was still wide open. He went in and headed straight for Eric's library. Eric had told him to look for the book – but which book? The library was full of books – they stretched from floor to ceiling on the shelves. George picked out a large heavy tome and looked at the cover. *Euclidean Quantum Gravity*, it said on the front. He flicked through the pages. He tried to read a little:

... because the retarded time co-ordinate goes to infinity on the event horizon, the surfaces of constant phase of the solution will pile up near the event horizon.

It was hopeless. He had no idea what any of it meant. He tried another book, this one called *Unified String Theories*. He read a line from it: *The equation for a conformal ...*

His brain hurt as he tried to make out what it meant. In the end he decided it meant he hadn't yet found the right book. He carried on looking around the library. *Find the book*, Eric had said. *Find my new book*. George stood in the middle of the library and thought very hard. With no Cosmos, no Eric and no Annie, it seemed terribly empty in that house. The only link George had to them now was a pink spacesuit, some tangled wires and these huge piles of science books.

Suddenly, he missed them all so terribly that he felt a sort of pain in his heart: he realized that if he didn't do something, he might never see any of them again. Cosmos had been stolen, Eric was fighting with a black hole and Annie would certainly never want to speak to him again if she thought George had anything to do with her dad getting lost for ever in outer space. He had to think of something.

He concentrated very hard. He thought of Eric and tried to imagine him with his new book in his hand – to picture the front cover so that he could remember what the book had been called. Where would he have put it? Suddenly George knew.

He ran into the kitchen and looked next to the teapot. Sure enough, there, covered in tea stains and rings where hot mugs had been rested on top of it, was a brand-new book called *Black Holes*, which, George now realized, was actually written by Eric himself! There was a sticker on it which read, in what must be Annie's handwriting: *Freddy the pig's favourite book!* with a little cartoon drawing of Freddy next to the words. *That's it!* thought George. *This must be the new book Eric was so happy to find when Freddy stormed through the house! This* must *be the one.*

There was just one more thing he needed from Eric's house – it was another book, a large one with lots and lots of pages. He grabbed it from beside the telephone, stripped off Annie's pink spacesuit and, shoving the two books into his school bag, rushed back to his own house, closing Eric's front door carefully behind him as he went.

That evening George scoffed his supper very quickly and then shot upstairs to his room, claiming he had lots of homework to do. First of all he got the very big book out of his bag. On the front it said: TELEPHONE DIRECTORY.

As his parents didn't have a phone, George had thought it was unlikely they would have the phone book, which was why he had borrowed Eric's. He searched through the alphabetical lists under 'R'. Using his finger to go down the long column of names, he came to REEPER, DR G., 42 FOREST WAY. George knew Forest Way – it was the road that led out of town to the woods where his parents took him in autumn to gather mushrooms and blackberries. He figured he couldn't go there tonight – it was too late and his parents would never let him out at this time. And anyway, he still had work to do with the *Black Holes* book. First thing in the morning, though, he'd go to Dr Reeper's house on his way to school. By then he hoped he would have a plan.

He put down the phone book and got Eric's *Black Holes* book out of his bag, desperately hoping it would hold the information he needed to rescue Eric. Every time he thought about Eric – which was about once every three minutes – he felt awful. He imagined him alone and frightened in outer space, not knowing how to get back, with a black hole trying to drag him into its dark belly.

George opened the book and read the first sentence of page one. *We are all in the gutter, but some of us are looking at the stars*, he read. It was a quote from the famous Irish writer Oscar Wilde. George felt it was written specially for him: he was indeed in the gutter, and he knew for sure that some people were looking at the stars. So he kept on reading, but that first sentence was the only one he understood. Next he read: *In 1916 Karl Schwarzschild found the first ever analytic black hole solution to Einstein's equation . . .*

Aarrgghh! he groaned to himself. The book was in a foreign language again! Why had Eric told him to look for this book? He didn't understand it at all. And Eric had written it! Yet every time Eric had told him about science, he had made it sound so simple, so easy to understand. George felt his eyes welling up. He'd failed them: Cosmos, Annie and Eric. He lay down on his bed with the book in his hand as hot tears ran down his cheeks. There was a tap at the door and his mum came in.

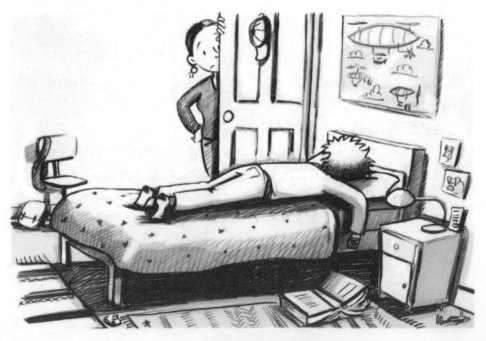

'Georgie,' she said, 'you look very pale, love. Are you feeling ill?'

'No, Mum,' he said sadly. 'I'm just finding my homework really difficult.'

'Well, I'm not surprised!' His mum had picked up the *Black Holes* book, which had fallen out of George's hand and onto the floor. She looked through it. 'It's a very difficult textbook for professional researchers! Honestly, I'm going to write to the school and tell them this is ridiculous.' As she spoke, a few pages fluttered out from the back of the book.

'Oh dear,' said George's mum, collecting them up, 'I'm dropping your notes.'

'They're not—' 'Mine' George was about to say when he stopped himself. At the top of one of the pages George read: *My Difficult Book Made Simple for Annie and George.*

'Thanks, Mum,' he said quickly, grabbing the pages off her. 'I think you've just found the bit I need. I'll be fine now.'

'Are you sure?' said his mum, looking rather surprised.

'Yes, Mum.' George nodded furiously. 'Mum, you're a star. Thank you.'

'A star?' said his mum, smiling. 'That's a nice thing to say, George.'

'No, really,' said George earnestly, thinking of Eric telling him that they were all the children of stars. 'You are.'

'And don't you work too hard, my little star,' George's mum told him, kissing him on the forehead. George was smiling now so she went off downstairs to put another batch of lentil cakes in the oven, feeling a lot happier about him.

As soon as his mum left the room, George jumped off his bed and gathered together all the bits of paper that had fallen out of the back of the *Black Holes* book. They were covered in spidery handwriting and little doodles and numbered pages 1–7. He started to read.

Chapter Twenty-Six

*M*y Difficult Book Made Simple for Annie and George
(version 3), it began.

WHAT YOU NEED TO KNOW
ABOUT BLACK HOLES

SECTION 1 *What is a black hole?*

SECTION 2 *How is a black hole made?*

SECTION 3 *How do you see a black hole?*

SECTION 4 *Falling into a black hole.*

SECTION 5 *Getting out of a black hole.*

SECTION 1

What is a Black Hole?

A black hole is a region where gravity is so strong that any light that tries to escape gets dragged back. Because nothing can travel faster than light, everything else will get dragged back too. So you can fall into a black hole and never get out again. A black hole has always been thought of as the ultimate prison from which there's no escape. Falling into a black hole is like falling over Niagara Falls: there's no way of getting back the same way you came.

The edge of a black hole is called the 'horizon'. It is like the edge of a waterfall. If you are above the edge, you can get away if you paddle fast enough, but once you pass the edge, you are doomed.

pulled faster + faster

As more things fall into a black hole, it gets bigger and the horizon moves further out. It is like feeding a pig. The more you feed it, the larger it gets.

SECTION 2

How is a Black Hole made?

To make a black hole you need to squash a very large amount of matter into a very small space. Then the pull of gravity will be so strong that light will be dragged back, unable to escape.

One way black holes are formed is when stars that have burned up their fuel explode like giant hydrogen bombs called supernovas. The explosion will drive off the outer layers of the star in a great expanding shell of gas and it will push the central regions inwards. If the star is more than a few times the size of our Sun, a black hole will form.

Much larger black holes are formed inside clusters and in the centre of galaxies. These regions will contain black holes and neutron stars as well as ordinary stars. Collisions between black holes and the other objects will produce a growing black hole that swallows anything that comes too near it. Our own galaxy, the Milky Way, has at its centre a black hole several million times the mass of our Sun.

NEUTRON STAR

When stars much more
massive than the Sun runs
out of fuel, they usually
expel all their outer layers
in a giant explosion called a
supernova. Such an explosion
is so powerful and bright it can
outshine the light of billions
and billions of
stars put together.

 But sometimes not everything is expelled in such an explosion. Sometimes the core of the star can remain behind as a ball. After a supernova explosion, this remnant is very hot: around 180,000 degrees Fahrenheit (100,000 degrees Celsius), but there is no more nuclear reaction to keep it hot.

Some remnants are so massive that under the influence of gravity they collapse in on themselves until they are only a few dozen miles across. For this to happen, these remnants need to have a mass that is between around 1.4 and 2.1 times the mass of the Sun.

The pressure is so intense inside these balls that they become liquid inside, surrounded by a solid crust about a mile (1.6 km) thick. The liquid is made of particles that normally remain inside the core of the atoms – the neutrons – so these balls are called neutron stars.

There are also other particles inside neutron stars, but they really consist mostly of neutrons. To create such a liquid on Earth is beyond our present technology.

Stars like the Sun do not explode in supernovae but become red giants whose remnants are not massive enough to shrink under their own gravity. These remnants are called white dwarfs. White dwarfs cool down over a period of billions of years, until they are not hot any more.

Many neutron stars have been observed by modern telescopes. Since the cores of stars are made of the heaviest elements forged inside stars (like iron), although white dwarfs can be quite small (about the size of the Earth) they are extremely heavy (about the mass of the Sun).

Star remnants that are less heavy than 1.4 times the mass of the Sun become white dwarfs. Neutron stars are born from supernovae remnants that have between 1.4 and 2.1 times the mass of the Sun. Remnants more massive than 2.1 times the size of the Sun never stop collapsing on themselves and become black holes.

SECTION 3

How Can You See a Black Hole?

The answer is, you can't because no light can get out of a black hole. It is like looking for a black cat in a black cellar. But you can detect a black hole by the way its gravity pulls on other things. We see stars that are orbiting something we can't see, but which we know can only be a black hole.

We also see discs of gas and dust rotating about a central object that we can't see, but which we know can only be a black hole.

gas

dust

SECTION 4

Falling into a Black Hole

normal astronaut

You can fall into a black hole just as you can fall into the Sun. If you fall in feet first, your feet will be nearer to the black hole than your head and will be pulled harder by the gravity of the black hole. So you will be stretched out lengthwise and squashed in sideways.

TO DO!
......
must buy for conference

tea
eggs
vanilla
biscuits
sugar
Jammy Dodgers
spaghetti

napkins
ginger biscuits

must call prof
CRZKZAK

BLACK HOLE

This stretching and squeezing is weaker the bigger the black hole is. If you fall into a black hole made by a star only a few times the size of our Sun, you will be torn apart and made into spaghetti before you even reach the black hole.

astronaut falling in a black hole →

But if you fall into a much bigger black hole, you will pass the horizon – the edge of the black hole and the point of no return – without noticing anything particular. However, someone watching you fall in from a distance will never see you cross the horizon because gravity warps time and space near a black hole. To them you will appear to slow down as you approach the horizon and get dimmer and dimmer. You get dimmer because the light you send out takes longer and longer to get away from the black hole. If you cross the horizon at 11:00 according to your wristwatch, someone looking at you would see the watch slow down and never quite reach 11:00.

spaghetti

falling

Stretched and squeezed sq until fatally

Spaghettified

horizon → point of no return

not quite 11:00

galileo

SECTION 5

Getting Out of a Black Hole

People used to think nothing could ever get out of a black hole. After all, that's why they were called black holes. Anything that fell into a black hole was thought to be lost and gone for ever; black holes would last until the end of time. They were eternal prisons from which there was no hope of escape.

LOST

DOOMED

But then it was discovered that this picture wasn't quite right. Tiny fluctuations in space and time meant that black holes couldn't be the perfect traps they were once thought; instead they would slowly leak particles in the form of Hawking Radiation. The rate of leakage is slower the bigger the black hole is.

b.h.

The Hawking Radiation would cause black holes to gradually evaporate. The rate of evaporation will be very slow at first but it will speed up as the black hole gets smaller. Eventually, after billions and billions of years, the black hole will

large black holes evaporate slowly.

the smaller black hole the quicker it evaporat

disappear. So black holes aren't eternal prisons after all. But what about their prisoners – the things that made the black hole or that fell in later? They will be recycled into energy and particles. But if you examine what comes out of the black hole very carefully, you can reconstruct what was inside. So the memory of what falls into a black hole is not lost for ever, just for a very long time.

YOU <u>CAN</u> GET OUT OF A BLACK HOLE!

Chapter Twenty-Seven

The next day was the day of the big science competition at school. George left home early. He said goodbye to his pig, kissed his mother, put Eric's book on black holes into his school bag and scooted out of the door, breakfast in hand. His dad offered to take him to school on the back of his bicycle-made-for-two but George just yelled, 'No thanks, Dad,' and was gone, leaving his parents feeling like a small tornado had just swept through the house.

George ran up the road, and when he got to the main junction, he looked back to see if either of his parents were waving at him from the front door. When he saw they weren't, he turned left at the corner instead of right, the direction he would have taken to go to school. He knew he didn't have much time so he hurried along as fast as he could. As he ran, thoughts streamed through his head.

He thought about Eric who, by now, would be swallowed up by the great dark menace of the black hole, the strongest force in the Universe. He thought about Cosmos and whether he would find him in the place where he was headed. He thought about Annie, who he would see later at the competition. Would she believe him when he told her that her dad had been tricked by an evil former colleague into taking a journey across outer space which had plunged him into great danger?

Now George understood why Annie told such extraordinary stories – after the wonders of the Universe, real life did seem pretty dull. He couldn't imagine a life without Annie or Cosmos or Eric now. Or at least he could, but he didn't want to. He had to save Eric, he *had* to!

George didn't know and couldn't imagine why Dr Reeper wanted to throw Eric into a black hole and make off with his amazing computer. But he could guess that whatever Dr Reeper was up to, it wasn't for the good of mankind, science, Eric or anyone else. Whatever Dr Reeper's aim was, George felt sure it was a horrible one.

The other thing that went through George's head as he ran on towards Dr Reeper's house was the science competition later that day. If he won the competition by giving a great talk about the Solar System, even his dad wouldn't be able to say no to George having the computer in the house. The problem was that the clever plan George had cooked up to save Eric from being eaten up by a black hole meant he wouldn't actually *be* at the competition. So he had no hope of winning. It wasn't easy for George to give up the idea of entering, but he knew he had no choice if he wanted to get Eric back. There was no other way to do it.

George reached 42 Forest Way and took a few moments to get his breath back. As he panted quietly, he looked at the house in front of him. The driveway led through some dilapidated gates to a huge old building with weird-looking turrets sticking out of the roof.

George crept up the drive to the house and stared in through a large window. Through the grimy glass he saw a room full of furniture covered in yellowing sheets and cobwebs hanging from the ceiling. Picking his way through a bed of nettles, he tiptoed to the next set of windows. One of the windows was just ajar at the bottom. Looking in, George saw a familiar sight.

In the middle of a crazed mess of pipes, cables and narrow glass tubes holding bubbling brightly coloured liquids was Dr Reeper, with his back to him, standing in front of a computer screen which was glowing with green light. Even from behind, George could tell that Dr Reeper was not at all happy. He watched as his teacher

struck the computer keyboard wildly, using all his fingers at once, as though playing a very difficult piano solo. The window was open just enough for George to hear what he was saying.

'*See!*' Dr Reeper yelled at the computer screen. 'I can keep doing this all day! Eventually I'll find the secret key, you just see if I don't! And when I do, you'll have to let me into the Universe! You'll have to!'

'Negative,' replied Cosmos. 'You have entered an incorrect command. I cannot process your request.'

Dr Reeper tried some different keys.

'Error,' said Cosmos. 'Error type two-nine-three.'

'Grrrrrrr!' cried Dr Reeper. 'I will crack you, Cosmos.

I will!' At that moment his phone rang. He snatched it up. 'Yes?' he barked into the receiver. 'Ahhh,' he went on in a more polite voice. 'Hello – you got my message?' He coughed in a very fake way. 'I'm not feeling so good today . . . No, just a bad cold . . . I think I'll have to take the day off . . . Such a shame about the competition . . .' He coughed a few more times. 'Sorry! Must dash – I'm feeling really ropey. *Byyyeee!*' He slammed the phone down and turned back to Cosmos. 'See, little computer!' he said, rubbing his hands. 'Now I have all *day*!'

'I do not operate for anyone who is not a member of the Order,' replied Cosmos, sounding very brave.

'Ha-ha-ha-ha!' Dr Reeper laughed madly. 'So the old Order still exists, does it? Those silly busybodies who think they can save the planet and humanity! The fools,' he went on. 'They should save themselves while there is still time. That's what *I* intend to do. Forget humanity! Humans don't deserve to be saved.' He spat on the floor. 'Look what they've done so far to this beautiful planet. I'm going to start again somewhere else, with a new life form. Those silly little boys think I'll be taking them with me. But I won't! Ha-ha-ha-ha! I'll leave them here to perish, like the rest of the human race. I'll be the only one left in the Universe, me and my new life form, which will obey my every word. All I need is to get out there, into outer space. You, Cosmos, are going to help me.'

'Negative,' replied Cosmos. 'I refuse to operate for a non-member of the Order.'

'I was a member once,' claimed Dr Reeper.

'Your membership was cancelled,' replied Cosmos firmly. 'After you—'

'Yes, yes, yes,' said Dr Reeper quickly. 'Let's not talk about that. Don't bring up bad memories now, Cosmos. Surely it's time to forgive and forget?' He spoke in a horrible, syrupy voice.

'Negative,' said Cosmos, causing Dr Reeper to rise up in a fury in front of the computer and bring his hands crashing down once more on the keyboard.

'Ouch,' said Cosmos, a few bright sparks flying out from the keyboard.

George couldn't bear to watch any longer. As much as he wanted to break in and stop Dr Reeper from hurting poor Cosmos any more, he knew it was vital to get him out of the house and away from the great computer as quickly as possible. To do that, George needed to get to school.

He ran back until he reached the school gates. Big coaches sat in the road outside, hordes of children wearing different-coloured school uniforms climbing out of them. These were the other kids from nearby schools arriving to take part in the science competition. George weaved through the crowds, saying, ''Scuse me, sorry, 'scuse me, sorry.' He was searching for someone.

'George!' He heard his name and looked around but couldn't see who was shouting at him. Then he spotted her – a tiny figure in a dark blue uniform, jumping up and down and waving at him. He scrambled over to her as quickly as he could.

'Annie!' he said when he reached her. 'I'm so glad to see you! Come on, we haven't got a minute to spare.'

'What's up?' said Annie, wrinkling her nose. 'Is something wrong with your talk?'

'Is that your boyfriend?' A much older boy in the same school uniform as Annie interrupted them.

'Oh, go away,' Annie snapped at the bigger boy. 'And say stupid things to someone else.' George held his breath in fear, waiting to see what the bigger boy would do. But he just turned away meekly and got lost in the crowd.

'Where've you been?' George asked Annie.

'I told you,' replied Annie. 'At Granny's house. Mum dropped me back at the school so I haven't even been home yet. What's wrong, George? What is it?'

'Annie,' said George very seriously, 'I've got something awful to tell you.' But he didn't get the chance. A teacher blew a whistle very loudly, forcing everyone to be quiet.

'Right!' the teacher announced. 'I want you all to line up in your school groups, ready to go into the great hall, where the science competition will begin. *You*' – he pointed at George in his dark green uniform among a crowd of kids in blue – 'are with the wrong school! Kindly go and find your own group before you confuse people any more!'

'Meet me just outside the hall!' George hissed to Annie. 'It's really important, Annie! I need your help!' With that he left her and joined his own school group. He started walking towards the hall, looking now for someone – or rather several someones – else. When he saw them – Ringo and his group of friends hovering in the corridor – George knew what he had to do. He grabbed the nearest teacher and started speaking in a very loud voice.

'Sir!' he yelled. '*Sir!*'

'What is it, George?' said the teacher, backing off a little at the unexpected volume.

'Sir!' shouted George again, making sure everyone around had stopped what they were doing and was listening to him. 'I need to change the topic of my talk!'

'I'm not sure that's possible,' said the teacher. 'And do you mind not shouting?'

'But I have to!' bellowed George. 'I've got a new title!'

'What's the title?' said the teacher, who was now worried that the boy had gone a bit potty.

'It's *Cosmos, the World's Most Amazing Computer, and How He Works.*'

'I see,' said the teacher, thinking George was definitely mad. 'I'll ask the judging panel what they think.'

'*Oh good, thank you, sir!*' George yelled even louder than before. 'Did you catch the whole title? It's *Cosmos, the World's Most Amazing Computer, and How He Works.*'

'Thank you, George,' said the teacher quietly. 'I'll do my best for you.'

As he walked off, sighing deeply to himself, George noticed that Ringo had taken out his mobile phone and was making a call. All he could do now was wait.

George stood by the entrance to the hall, watching the long lines of schoolchildren file in past him. He didn't

have to wait long before, out of breath and trembling with excitement, Dr Reeper rushed up to him.

'George!' he exclaimed, smoothing his hair down with one scaly hand. 'Did you manage? To change the topic of your talk, that is?'

'I think so,' George told him.

'I'll check for you,' said Dr Reeper. 'Don't worry, you go ahead and give the talk on Cosmos and how he works and I'll make sure it's OK with the judging panel. Good idea for a talk, George. Brilliant!'

Just then the headteacher came past. 'Reeper?' he said curiously. 'I heard you were ill today.'

'I'm feeling *much* better,' stated Dr Reeper firmly. 'And very much looking forward to the competition.'

'That's the spirit!' said the head. 'I'm so glad you're here, Reeper! One of the judges has had to drop out so you're just the chap to take his place.'

True-colour image of the Andromeda galaxy. It is the closest major galaxy to our own and the largest in terms of the number of stars it contains. Like the Milky Way, it is a spiral galaxy. Light takes about 150,000 years to travel across Andromeda, and 2.5 million years to reach the Earth.

Computer-enhanced image of a possible extrasolar planet (in red) orbiting around a very hot ball that is not big enough to become a star (in white). The planet is thought to be five times the mass of Jupiter, and this picture could be the first exoplanet image ever taken.

Optical image of a giant elliptical galaxy named NGC 4261 (centre). At the galaxy's core there is a supermassive black hole about half a billion times bigger than our Sun.

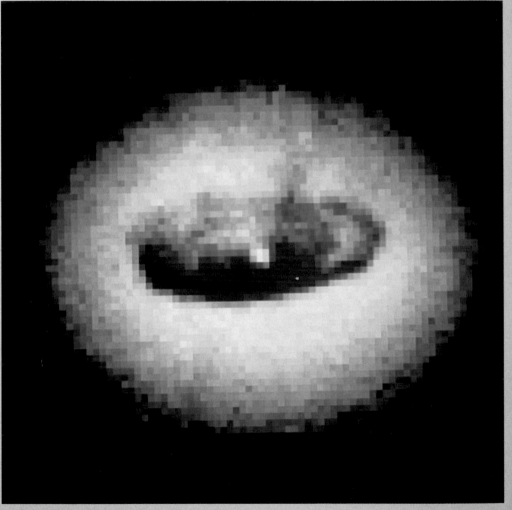

© NASA/ESA/STSCI/F. FERRARESE, JHU/ SCIENCE PHOTO LIBRARY

Centre of NGC 4261 (see previous page). Surrounding the black hole is a disc of cold dark dust approximately 800 light years in width. It is believed that there is a massive or supermassive black hole at the core of most galaxies.

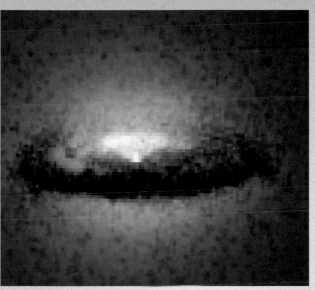

© NASA/ESA/STSCI/R. VAN DER MAREL/SCIENCE PHOTO LIBRARY

This ring of dust hides a massive black hole at the centre of another galaxy called NGC 7052. The bright white spot at the centre is light from stars crowded around the black hole due to its powerful gravitational pull.

This prominent blue jet is streaming out from the core of a giant elliptical galaxy called M87. The jet is made of electrons and other particles accelerated from around a supermassive black hole at the centre of that galaxy.

© NASA/ESA/STSCI/HUBBLE HERITAGE TEAM/ SCIENCE PHOTO LIBRARY

Computer artwork of the Solar System. Shown here: a section of the Sun (on left); the eight planets (L–R): Mercury, Venus, Earth, Mars, Jupiter, Saturn, Uranus and Neptune; and the three dwarf planets, in red boxes (L–R): Ceres, Pluto and Eris. The distance between the objects is not to scale or nothing would be seen except the Sun; however, the relative sizes are correct.

A satellite image of the Earth.

'Oh no no no no no no no no no,' said Dr Reeper hurriedly. 'I'm sure you can find someone much better.'

'Poppycock!' said the head. 'You're just the ticket! Come along, Reeper, you can sit with me.'

Grimacing, Reeper had no choice but to follow the headteacher and take a seat next to him at the front of the hall.

George waited by the door until at last he saw Annie again, coming towards him in a great gaggle of kids in blue uniforms. As she walked past him, he grabbed her sleeve and pulled her out of the great river of children flowing into the hall.

'We've got to go!' he whispered in her ear. '*Now!*'

'Where?' asked Annie. 'Where have we got to go?'

'Your dad's fallen into a black hole!' said George. 'Follow me – we have to rescue him . . .'

Chapter Twenty-Eight

Annie hurried along the corridor after George.
'But, George,' she said, 'where are we going?'

'Shush,' he said over his shoulder. 'This way.' He was taking Annie towards the side door, which led out onto the road. It was strictly forbidden for pupils to go out of that door by themselves during school hours. If George and Annie were caught leaving school without permission, they would be in deep trouble. Worse – much worse – they would forfeit their only chance to reach Cosmos, which would mean that Eric would be lost inside a black hole for ever. It was vital that they got out of the school as fast as possible.

They walked along stiffly, trying to look completely natural and innocent, as though they had every reason in the world to be going in the opposite direction to everyone else. It seemed to be working – no one paid them any attention. They were just approaching the side door when George saw a teacher walking towards them. He crossed his fingers, hoping they wouldn't be spotted, but it didn't work.

'George,' said the teacher. 'And where might you be going?'

'Oh, sir!' said George. 'We, um, we are just, um . . .' He faltered and ran out of steam.

'I left something for the science presentation in my coat pocket, sir,' Annie's clear voice cut in. 'So my teacher asked this boy to show me the way back to the cloakrooms.'

'Carry on, then,' said the teacher, letting them pass. But he stood watching them until they disappeared into the cloakrooms. When they peered back down the corridor, he was still standing there, guarding the school

exit. The last children were straggling into the science presentation, which was due to start any minute now.

'Rats,' said George, retreating back into the cloakroom. 'We won't get out through that door.' They looked around. In the wall above the rows of coat pegs was a long thin rectangular window.

'Do you think you can squeeze through?' George asked Annie.

'It's the only way out, isn't it?' she said, gazing up at the window.

George nodded grimly.

'Then I'll just have to,' said Annie with great determination. 'I'm not letting a black hole eat my dad, I'm not, I'm not, I'm not!'

George could tell by the way she screwed up her face that she was trying not to cry. He wondered if he'd done the right thing in telling her – maybe he should have tried to rescue Eric all by himself? But it was too late for these kinds of thoughts. He had Annie with him now and they needed to get on with it.

'Come on then,' he said

briskly. 'I'll give you a leg up.' He hoisted her up so she could undo the catch, push the window open and slither through the narrow gap; she gave a small squeak as she vanished from view. George pulled himself up onto the ledge and tried to slide through as Annie had done, but he was a lot bigger than her and it wasn't easy. He got halfway through but then couldn't go any further! He was stuck, one side of him dangling out of the window over the street outside his school, the other still inside the cloakroom.

'George!' Annie reached up and grabbed his foot.

'Don't pull!' he said, gently easing himself through the gap, sucking in his breath as much as he could. With another wriggle, he pulled himself free of the tight frame and landed in a crumpled heap on the pavement. He staggered to his feet and grabbed Annie's hand. 'Run!' he panted. 'We've got to get out of sight.'

They sped round the corner and stopped so that George could get his breath back. 'Annie—' he started to say, but she waved at him to be quiet. She'd got out her mobile phone and was making a call.

'Mum!' she said urgently into the phone. 'It's an emergency . . . No, I'm fine, it's not me . . . Yes, I'm at the school where you dropped me this morning but I've got to . . . No, Mum, I haven't done anything . . . Mum, listen, *please*! Something's happened to Dad, something awful, and we've got to rescue him . . . He's gone into outer space and got lost and we have to get him back . . . Can you come and collect us? I'm with my friend George and we're just near his school. Quickly, Mum, quickly, hurry up, we haven't got long . . . OK, bye.'

'What did your mum say?' asked George.

'She said, *When will your father learn to stop doing silly things and behave like an adult?*'

'What does she mean by that?' said George, rather perplexed.

'I don't know,' said Annie. 'Grown-ups have funny ideas.'

'Is she coming?'

'Yes. She won't be long – she's coming in her Mini.'

Sure enough, just a few minutes later a little red car with white stripes pulled up next to them. A sweet-faced lady with long brown hair wound down the window and stuck her head out.

'Well, whatever next!' she said cheerfully. 'Your father and his adventures! I don't know. And what are you two doing out of school?'

'George, this is my mum. Mum this is George,' said Annie, ignoring her mother's question and wrenching

open the passenger door. She held the front seat forward
so that George could climb in. 'You can go in the back,'
she told him. 'But be careful, don't break anything.' The
back seat was covered in recorders, cymbals, triangles,
mini-harps and string drums.

'Sorry, George,' said Annie's mum as he clambered
in. 'I'm a music teacher – that's why I have so many
instruments.'

'A music teacher?' echoed George in surprise.

'Yes,' said Annie's mum. 'What did Annie tell you I
was? President of the United States?'

'No,' said George, catching her eye in the rear-view
mirror. 'She said you were a dancer in Moscow.'

'That's enough talking about me as though I wasn't

here,' said Annie, putting on her seat belt. 'Mum – drive the car! We *need* to rescue Dad, it's really important.'

Annie's mum just sat there with the engine off. 'Don't panic, Annie,' she said mildly. 'Your father's been in all sorts of difficult situations before. I'm sure he's going to be fine. After all, Cosmos wouldn't let anything terrible happen to him. I think you two should go back to school and we won't say any more about it.'

'Um, that's the thing,' said George, who wasn't quite sure what to call Annie's mum. 'Eric hasn't got Cosmos – he's been stolen! Eric's in outer space all by himself. And he's near a black hole.'

'By himself?' repeated Annie's mum. She suddenly turned quite pale. 'No Cosmos? But then he can't get back! And a black hole . . . ?'

'Mum, I keep telling you it's an emergency!' pleaded Annie. 'Now do you believe me?'

'Oh my goodness gracious me! Fasten your seat belt, George!' exclaimed Annie's mum, starting the car. 'And tell me where I need to go.'

George gave her Dr Reeper's address and she put her foot down on the accelerator so hard that the little car shot forward with a great lurch.

As the red Mini zoomed through the heavy traffic towards Greeper's house, George explained as best he could what had happened over the past twenty-four hours. While the little car wove through the traffic across town, nipping in and out – much to annoyance of people in bigger cars – he told Annie and her mum (who asked him to call her Susan) all about going to see Eric yesterday to ask for his help with his science presentation.  He told them about the mysterious note that he hadn't trusted and Eric leaping through the portal into outer space and having to follow him. And how both of them had got sucked towards an invisible force and how when the doorway appeared to save them, it was too faint and only George had managed to get through.

He told them about landing in the library and looking round to find that Eric wasn't there, and how Cosmos had been stolen; how George had run after the thieves but had lost them in the dark; how he had gone back to Eric's to look for the book that Eric had told him to find; how he'd tried to read it but couldn't understand it and then had found the notes in the back which explained that it *was* possible to escape from a black hole; how he needed to find Cosmos because although someone *could* escape from a black hole, he would need Cosmos to make it happen; and how he'd realized where Cosmos must be and had gone there that morning and seen Dr Reeper—

'Reeper? Do you mean Graham Reeper?' Susan interrupted him as she swerved the little car round a corner.

'Yes,' replied George. 'Greeper. He's my teacher. Do you know him?'

'I did once, a long time ago,' said Susan in a dark voice. 'I always told Eric that he shouldn't trust Graham. But he wouldn't listen. Eric always thought the best of people. Until. . .' She trailed off.

'Until what?' piped up Annie. 'Until what, Mum?'

'Until something terrible happened,' said Susan, her mouth set in a grim line. 'Something none of us have ever forgotten.'

'None of who?' said Annie, gasping with excitement at the prospect of a thrilling family story she hadn't heard before. But she didn't get to find out, as right then her mum turned into Greeper's driveway and parked the car in front of his house.

Chapter Twenty-Nine

It wasn't easy to break into Greeper's house. Even though the place was old, scruffy and unloved, Greeper had locked every single window and door. They went around the house, trying everywhere, but nothing would budge. When they reached the window of the room where George had seen Cosmos only that morning, it looked like the great computer was no longer there.

'But I saw him!' protested George. 'In that room!'

Annie and Susan looked at each other. Susan bit her lip to try and hide her disappointment. A fat tear snaked down Annie's cheek.

'If we can't find Cosmos . . .' she whispered.

'Hang on a minute!' exclaimed Susan. 'Shush, you two! Listen!' They all strained their ears as hard as they could.

From somewhere inside the room they heard the faint tinny mechanical sound of someone singing: '*Hey diddle diddle the cat and the fiddle . . . the cow jumped over the moon . . .* although technically that would not be possible without a spacesuit because the cow would freeze,' the voice added.

'It's Cosmos!' cried George. 'He's singing so that we know where to find him! But how are we going to get to him?'

'Wait there!' said Susan mysteriously. She vanished off round the corner, but a few minutes later appeared inside the room where Cosmos was singing. She opened the ground-floor window very wide so that Annie and George could climb through.

'How did you do that?' asked George in wonder.

'I should have thought of it before,' said Susan. 'Graham had left his spare key under a flowerpot by the front door. It's what he always used to do. So I let myself in.'

Meanwhile Annie had followed the sound of brave Cosmos's singing and was rootling around in a big cupboard. She pulled out a cardboard box full of old blankets, threw them out and, at the bottom, found Cosmos himself. Unfolding his screen, she covered it in kisses. 'Cosmos, Cosmos, Cosmos!' she squealed. 'We found you! Are you all right? Can you rescue my dad?'

'Please plug me in,' gasped Cosmos, who was a bit the worse for wear. At Eric's house, he had been sleek, silver and shiny – a glossy, well-looked-after computer. Now he was scratched and battered, with marks and smudges all over him. 'I am exhausted. My batteries are nearly flat.'

George looked at the spot where he had seen Cosmos earlier that day and, sure enough, there was the computer's cable. He attached Cosmos to the cable and heard him give big thirsty gulps, as though he was drinking down a huge glass of cold water.

'That's better!' sighed Cosmos. 'Now, would someone like to tell me what the microchip is going on around here?'

'Eric's fallen into a black hole!' George told him.

'And we need you to get him out,' pleaded Annie. 'Dear Cosmos, please say you know how.'

Cosmos made a whirring noise. 'I am checking my disks for information,' he said. 'I am searching for files on how to rescue someone from a black hole . . . Please wait . . .' He made more whirring noises and then stopped and went silent.

'Well?' said Annie, sounding worried. 'Can you?'

'Um, no,' said Cosmos reluctantly. 'Those search terms have produced zero information.'

'You don't know how? But, Cosmos, that means—' Annie couldn't finish the sentence. She threw her arms around her mum and started to cry.

'No one has provided me with information about escaping from black holes,' explained Cosmos apologetically. 'I only know how to get into a black hole and not how to get out again. I am not sure it is possible. Eric would have told me if he knew. I am accessing my archive on black holes, gravity and mass, but I fear none of these files holds the data I need.' His drives whirred again, but then he fell silent – unusually, for Cosmos, lost for words . . .

'So Eric's lost,' said Annie's mum, wiping her eyes. 'He told me a long time ago that nothing can come out of a black hole once it has fallen in.'

'No!' said George. 'That's not right! I mean, Eric's changed his mind about black holes. That's what he says in the notes he wrote for me and Annie.'

'What notes?' asked Cosmos.

'The ones I found in the back of his new book.'

'What did the notes say?'

Searching in his bag, George tried to remember Eric's exact words. 'Eric wrote that black holes are not eternal,' he said. 'They somehow spit out everything that falls in . . . takes a long time . . . radiator something.'

'Radiation,' corrected Cosmos. 'Do you have the book? Maybe I can download the information from it and work something out.'

'Yeah! Radiation! That's it!' George had found Eric's big book on black holes and handed it over to Annie. 'But, Cosmos, we've got to be quick – as soon as Greeper sees I'm not at school to give my talk, he'll come straight back here.'

'We'd be a lot quicker if Eric had bothered to update my system properly in the first place,' sniffed Cosmos.

'Perhaps he meant to but forgot?' said George.

'Typical!' said Cosmos.

'Do you mind?' said Annie crossly. 'Could we hurry up?'

'Of course,' said Cosmos, sounding serious again. 'Once I have the new information, I can start right away. Annie, attach the book to my book port.'

As quickly as she could, Annie pulled out a clear plastic tray from Cosmos's side and adjusted it until it stood upright. She propped the book on it and pressed a button on the computer. 'Ready?' she said.

The humming noise of the computer grew louder and louder and the pages of the book started to glow. 'Rebooting my memory files on black holes!' said Cosmos. 'Finished! You were right, George. It *is* all in Eric's new book. I *can* do it. I can rescue Eric from a black hole.'

'Then *do it*!' George, Annie and her mum shouted in unison.

Annie pressed the ENTER key on Cosmos's keyboard and the portal window appeared in the middle of the room. On the other side of it was a very distorted view of somewhere in outer space. In the middle was a black patch.

'That's the black hole!' cried George.

'Correct,' replied Cosmos. 'That's where I left you and Eric.'

The view seemed very still, as though nothing was happening.

'Cosmos, why aren't you doing anything?' asked Annie.

'It takes time,' replied Cosmos. 'I need to pick up all the little things that come out of the black hole. Most of them are so small you can't even see them. If I miss one, I may not be able to reconstruct Eric. I will have to filter out Eric from every single object that ever fell in the black hole.'

'What do you mean *reconstruct*?' asked Annie's mum.

'The black hole expels particles one by one. Each time a particle gets out, the black hole expels more the next time, so it gets quicker and quicker all the time. I'm fast forwarding time by billions of years. Please let me work. I need to pick up everything.'

George, Annie and her mum fell silent and stared through the window, each willing Cosmos to get it right. After a few minutes the black hole still looked exactly the same as it had before. But then, as they watched, it started to shrink, and the space around it became less and less distorted. Once the black hole had begun shrinking, it got smaller and smaller faster and faster. Now they could see an enormous number of particles which seemed to be coming from the black hole itself.

Cosmos was making a whirring noise that was getting louder and louder as the black hole shrank. The lights on his screen – so bright just a minute ago – started to flicker and grow dim. The whirring noise suddenly went crunchy and a high-pitched alarm rang out from Cosmos's keyboard.

'What's wrong with Cosmos?' George whispered to Annie and Susan.

Susan looked worried. 'It must be all the effort he's making with the calculations. Even for Cosmos, they must be very difficult.'

'Do you think he'll be able to do it?' squeaked Annie.

'We just have to hope,' said Susan firmly.

Through the window, they saw that the black hole was now the size of a tennis ball. 'Don't look!' cried Susan. 'Cover your eyes with your hands!' The black hole became very bright and then suddenly exploded, disappearing in the most powerful explosion the Universe could withstand. Even with their eyes closed, George, Annie and her mum could see its light.

'Hold on, Cosmos!' shouted Annie.

Cosmos gave a horrible groan and shot a green blaze of light out from his screen as some white smoke rose from his circuits. '*Eu-re-k—!*' Cosmos started to shout, but his voice was cut off before he reached the end of the word.

The light suddenly vanished, and when George opened his eyes, he saw that the window was no longer there. Instead, the portal doorway had appeared. It burst open and the room in Dr Reeper's house was flooded with the fading flash of brilliant light from the explosion. Standing in the middle of the doorway was the figure of a man in a spacesuit. Behind him, the portal doorway opened on a quiet place in space where the black hole was no more.

Chapter Thirty

Eric took off his helmet and shook himself, like a dog after a swim.

'That's better!' he said. He looked around. 'But where am I? And what happened?' A pair of spectacles with yellow glass in the frames slid off his nose and he looked at them in bemusement. 'These aren't mine!' He glanced at Cosmos but Cosmos's screen was blank and black smoke drifted from the keyboard.

Annie rushed forward and hugged him. 'Dad!' she squealed. 'You fell into a black hole! And George had to rescue you – he was so clever, Dad. He found out from the notes you left him that you could escape from the black hole,

272

but first he had to find Cosmos – Cosmos was stolen by a horrible man who—'

'Slow down, Annie, slow down!' said Eric, who seemed rather dazed. 'You mean I've been inside a black hole and come back again? But that's incredible! That means I've got it right – that means all the work I've done on black holes is correct. Information that goes into a black hole is *not* lost for ever – I know that now! That's amazing. Now, if I can come out of—'

'Eric!' said Susan sharply.

Eric jumped. 'Oh, Susan!' he said, looking rather sheepish and embarrassed. He handed over the yellow glasses. 'I don't suppose,' he said apologetically, 'you have a spare pair of my glasses with you? I seem to have come out of the black hole wearing someone else's.'

'These two have been running around all over town to try and save you,' said Susan, digging into her handbag and pulling out a pair of Eric's usual spectacles. 'They've played truant from school and George is missing the science competition he wanted to enter, all for your sake. I think the least you could do is say thank you, especially to George. He worked it all out by himself, you know

– about Graham and the black hole and everything else. And don't lose this pair!'

'Thank you, Annie,' said Eric, patting his daughter gently and putting his glasses onto his nose at their familiar wonky angle. 'And thank you, George. You've been very brave and very clever.'

'That's all right.' George stared at his feet. 'It wasn't me really – it was Cosmos.'

'No, it wasn't,' said Eric. 'Cosmos couldn't have got me back without you – otherwise I'd be here already, wouldn't I?'

'S'pose so,' said George rather gruffly. 'Is Cosmos all right?' The great computer was still silent and black-screened.

Eric untangled himself from Annie and went over to Cosmos. 'Poor old thing,' he said, unplugging the computer, folding him up and tucking him under his

arm. 'I expect he needs a bit of a rest. Now I'd better get home straight away and write up my new discoveries. I must let all the other scientists know immediately that I've made the most astonishing—'

Susan coughed loudly and glared at him.

Eric looked at her, puzzled. 'What?' he mouthed.

'George!' she mouthed back.

'Oh, of course!' said Eric out loud, striking his hand against his forehead. He turned to George. 'I'm so sorry! What I meant to say was that first of all I think we should go back to your school and see if you're still in time to enter the science competition. Is that right?' he asked Susan, who nodded and smiled.

'But I'm not sure . . .' protested George.

'We can go through your presentation in the car,' said Eric firmly. He started clanking towards the door in his spacesuit. 'Let's get moving.' He looked round to find that no one was following him.

'What now?' he asked, raising his eyebrows.

'Dad!' said Annie in tones of disgust. 'You're not going to George's school dressed like that, are you?'

'I don't think anyone will notice,' said Eric. 'But if you insist . . .' He peeled off his spacesuit to reveal his ordinary everyday clothes below, then ruffled his hair. 'And anyway, where are we? I don't recognize this place.'

'This, Eric,' said Susan, 'is Graham Reeper's house. Graham wrote you that note to send you into outer space, and while you were there, he stole Cosmos, thinking this would mean you could never come back.'

'No!' Eric gasped. 'Graham did it deliberately? He stole Cosmos?'

'I told you he'd never forgive you.'

'Oh dear,' said Eric sadly, struggling to pull off his space boot. 'That is very unhappy news.'

'Um, Eric,' piped up George, 'what did happen with you and Greeper? I mean, why did he want you to be eaten by a black hole? And why won't he ever forgive you?'

'Oh, George,' said Eric, shaking off the space boot, 'it's a long story. You know that Graham and I used to work together?' He reached into the inside pocket of his jacket for his wallet. From it he took out a crumpled old

photo and handed it to George. In the picture George saw two young men; standing in between them was an older man with a long white beard. Both the young men were wearing black gowns with white fur-lined hoods and all three were laughing at the camera. The man on the right had thick dark hair and heavy-framed glasses which, even then, were sitting at a slightly strange angle.

'But that's you!' said George, pointing at the photo. He examined the face of the other young man. It was strangely familiar. 'And that looks like Greeper! But he looks really nice and friendly, not scary and weird like he is now.'

'Graham,' said Eric quietly, 'was my best friend. We studied physics together at the university, the one here in this town. The man you see in the middle was our tutor – a brilliant cosmologist. He invented the concept of Cosmos, and Graham and I worked together on the early prototypes. We wanted a machine that would help us to explore outer space so that we could extend our knowledge of the Universe.

'At the beginning, Graham and I got along very well together,' Eric continued, gazing into the distance. 'But after a while he became strange and cold. I started to realize he wanted Cosmos all for himself. He didn't want to go on a quest for knowledge to benefit humanity – he wanted to use Cosmos to make himself rich and powerful by exploiting the wonders of space for his own good. You have to understand,' he added, 'that in those days, Cosmos was very different. Back then he was a gigantic computer – so big he took up a whole basement. And yet he wasn't even half as powerful as he is now. Anyway, one evening when Graham thought he was alone, I caught him. He was trying to use Cosmos for his own terrible ends. I was there and I tried to stop him and . . . it was . . . dreadful. Everything had to change after that.' Eric fell silent.

'What – after the terrible thing happened?' asked Annie.

Susan nodded. 'Yes, love,' she said. 'Don't ask your father any more questions about it. That's enough for now.'

Chapter Thirty-One

Back at George's school, the pupils in the hall were getting restless and bored. Kids were shifting around in their seats, whispering and giggling as a series of nervous, solemn-faced competitors from the different schools battled to gain their attention. However, no one was more agitated or jumpy than Dr Reeper, who was sitting in the front row with the headteacher and the other judges.

'Do sit still, Reeper! Good heavens, man!' hissed the head out of the side of his mouth. He was feeling very irritated with Dr Reeper for behaving so badly in front of the teachers and headteachers from the other schools. So far he hadn't bothered to listen to any of the presentations and hadn't asked a single question. All he had done was anxiously check the running order in his programme and crane his neck round to look at the hall behind him.

'I'll just go and make sure George is up to speed with his speech,' Reeper whispered back to the head.

'*You will not!*' spluttered the head. 'George will do perfectly well without you. Try and show some interest, would you? You're letting the school down.'

The boy on stage finished his speech on dinosaur remains. 'So that,' he concluded brightly to his tired audience, 'is how we know that dinosaurs first walked the Earth two hundred and thirty million years ago.' The teachers dutifully clapped as he clambered down from the stage and went back to join his school group.

The head stood up. 'And now,' he said, reading from his notes, 'we have our last contestant, our own George Greenby, from this very school! Can we give a big welcome to George, whose topic today is . . .' The head paused and read his notes again.

'No, no, that's correct,' said Dr Reeper hurriedly. He stood up. 'George's talk will be on the subject of Cosmos, the world's most amazing computer, and how he works. Hurray for George!' he cheered, but no one joined in. Then a long silence followed as everyone waited for George to appear. When he didn't, the noise level in the room rose as the kids, sensing the prospect of a swift end to the school day, rumbled with excitement.

The headteacher looked at his watch. 'I'll give him two minutes,' he said to the other judges. 'If he hasn't shown up by then, he'll be disqualified and we'll get on with the prize-giving.' Just like the pupils, the headteacher was thinking how nice it would be to get home early for once,

so he could have a cup of tea and a piece of cake and put his feet up with no pesky kids getting in the way.

The clock ticked round but still there was no sign of George. With just seconds to go, the head turned to the judges and was about to announce the competition closed when a flurry of activity at the back of the hall caught his attention. A group of people seemed to have come in – two adults, one with a laptop computer under his arm, a blonde girl and a boy.

The boy ran straight up to the front of the hall and said, 'Sir, am I still in time?'

'Yes, George,' said the head, relieved that he had shown up after all. 'Get yourself onto the stage. Good luck! We're relying on you!'

George climbed onto the big school stage and stood right in the very middle.

'Hello, everyone,' he said in a thin voice. The crowds in the hall ignored him and carried on pushing and pulling and pinching each other. 'Hello,' George tried again. For a moment he felt sick with nerves and very foolish, standing there by himself. But then he remembered what Eric had said to him in the car on the way there and he felt more confident. He pulled himself up straight, threw his arms out to either side and yelled, '*Good afternoon, Alderbash School!*'

The kids in the audience fell silent in surprise.

'*I said,*' bellowed George again, '*Good afternoon, Alderbash School!*'

'*Good afternoon, George!*' the room shouted back at him.

'Can you hear me at the back?' asked George in a loud voice. Leaning on the wall at the back of the hall, Eric gave him the thumbs up.

'My name,' continued George, 'is George Greenby. And I am here today to give a talk. The title of my talk is *My Secret Key to the Universe.*'

'Noooooo!' cried Dr Reeper, jumping out of his seat. 'That's wrong!'

'*Hush!*' said the head angrily.

'I'm leaving!' said Dr Reeper in a furious temper. He tried to storm out of the hall but got halfway down the centre aisle when he saw Eric standing at the back. Eric gave him a little wave, smiled and patted Cosmos, who he was carrying under his arm. Reeper turned a shade of light green and slunk back to his seat at the front, where he sat down quietly once more.

'You see,' George carried on, 'I've been really lucky. I found a secret key that's unlocked the Universe for me. Because of this secret key, I've been able to find out all sorts of things about the Universe around us. So I thought I'd share some of the stuff I learned with you. Because it's all about where we came from – what made us, what made our planet, our Solar System, our Galaxy, our Universe – and it's about our future. Where are we going? And what do we need to do to survive centuries into the future?

'I wanted to tell you about it because science is really important. Without it, we don't understand anything, so how can we get anything right or make any good decisions? Some people think science is boring, some people think it's dangerous – and if we don't get interested in science and learn about it and use it properly, then maybe it *is* those things. But if you try and understand it, it's fascinating and it matters to us and to the future of our planet.'

Everyone was listening to George now. When he stopped talking, there was complete silence.

He started again. 'Billions of years ago, there were clouds of gas and dust wandering in outer space. At first these clouds were very spread out and scattered, but over time, gravity helping, they started to shrink and become denser and denser . . .'

EARTH

☻ Earth is the third closest planet to the Sun.

☻ Average distance to the Sun: 93 million miles (149.6 million km)

70.8% of the surface of the Earth is covered with liquid water and the rest is divided into seven continents. These are: Asia (29.5% of the land surface of the Earth), Africa (20.5%), North America (16.5%), South America (12%), Antarctica (9%), Europe (7%) and Australia (5%). This definition of continents is mostly cultural since, for instance, no water expanse divides Asia from Europe. Geographically, there are only four continents that are not separated by water: Eurasia-Africa (57% of the land surface), Americas (28.5%), Antarctica (9%) and Australia (5%). The remaining 0.5% is made up of islands, mostly scattered within Oceania in the central and South Pacific.

☻ A day on Earth is divided into 24 hours, but in fact it takes Earth 23 hours, 56 minutes and 4 seconds to rotate around itself. There is a 3 minute and 56 seconds mismatch. Over a year this adds up to the one turn the Earth makes by going around its orbit.

☻ An Earth-year is the time it takes for the Earth to complete one revolution around the Sun. It may vary very slightly over time, but remains around 365.25 days.

☻ So far, the Earth is the only known planet in the Universe to harbour life.

Surface: 316,954,764 square miles (510,065,600 square km)

Diameter at equator: 7,926 miles (12,756 km)

Chapter Thirty-Two

'*So what?* you might think,' continued George. 'What's a cloud of dust got to do with anything? Why do we care or need to know what happened billions of years ago in outer space? Does it matter? Well, yes, it does. Because that cloud of dust is the reason we are here today.

'Now we know that stars are formed from giant clouds of gas in outer space. Some of these stars end their lives by becoming black holes that slowly, very slowly, let things escape until they vanish in a huge explosion.

'Other stars explode before they become black holes and send all the matter inside them through space. We know that all the elements we are made of were created inside the bellies of these stars that exploded a long time ago. All the people on Earth, the animals, the plants, the rocks, the air and the oceans are made of elements forged inside stars. Whatever we might think, we are all the children of stars. It took billions and billions of years for Nature to make us out of these elements.'

George paused for a second.

'So you see, it took an incredibly long time to make us and our planet. And our planet isn't like any other planet in the Solar System. There are bigger ones and more impressive ones but they aren't places you could think of as home. Like Venus, for example, which is really  hot. Or Mercury, where one day lasts for fifty-nine of our Earth days. Imagine that, if one day at school lasted fifty-nine days! That would be pretty awful.'

George paused for a moment and then continued to speak, the whole hall hanging on his every word as he described some of the wonders of the Solar System. Finally he came to what he thought was probably the most important bit at the end of his presentation.

'Our planet is amazing and it's ours,' he summed up. 'We belong to it – we're all made of the same stuff as the planet itself. We really do need to look after it. My dad's been saying this for years but I've just felt embarrassed by him. All I could see was how different he was from other parents. But I don't feel that way now – he's right to say we must stop messing up the Earth. And he's right that we can all try just a little bit harder. I feel proud of him now for wanting to protect something as unique and beautiful as the Earth. But we all need to do it or it won't work and our lovely planet will be ruined.

'Of course, we can also work on finding another planet for us to live on, but it isn't going to be easy. We know there isn't one close to us. So if there is another Earth out there – and there might be – it's a long long way away. It's exciting, trying to discover new planets and new worlds out there in the Universe. But that doesn't mean that home isn't the place you still want to come back to. We've got to make sure that in a hundred years' time, we've still got an Earth to return to.

'So you might wonder how I know all this. Well, the other thing I wanted to say to you is that you don't need to find an actual secret key, like I did, to unlock the Universe and help the Earth. There's one that everyone can use, if they learn how. It's called "physics". That's what you need to understand the Universe around you. Thank you!'

The hall burst into applause as everyone rose to their feet to give George a standing ovation. Wiping a tear from his eye, the headteacher sprang onto the stage to clap George on the back and said, 'Well done, George! Well done!' He pumped George's arm up and down in a very vigorous handshake. George blushed. He was embarrassed by the clapping and wished it would stop.

Down in the audience, Dr Reeper also appeared to be crying, but not from pride or happiness, like the head.

He was weeping for quite a different reason. 'Cosmos!' he raged under his breath. 'So close! I had you in my hands! And now he's stolen you away from me!'

The headteacher helped George down off the platform and had a very brief consultation with his fellow judges – all except Dr Reeper, that is, who was hunched in his seat whispering to himself and casting nasty looks at George. Borrowing the PT teacher's whistle and blowing it sharply several times, the head brought the hall to order again.

'Er-hum!' he said, clearing his throat. 'I would like to announce that this year's winner of the inter-school science presentation is, by – almost! – a unanimous vote on the part of the judges, *George Greenby*!' The school hall cheered. 'George,' the head carried on, 'has given us a wonderful presentation and I am delighted to award him the first prize, which is this truly amazing computer, kindly donated by our sponsors.' One of the other judges produced a large cardboard box from under the table and handed it to George.

'Thank you, sir, thank you!' said George, who was rather overwhelmed, both by the experience and by the size of the box he had just been given. He staggered down the centre aisle towards the exit, clasping his prize in both hands. Everyone smiled as he passed – except for one group of boys sitting on the end of the row, who were deliberately not clapping. They sat there with their arms folded, glaring at George.

'You haven't heard the last of this,' hissed Ringo as George drew level with him.

George ignored him and hurried on until he reached Eric, Annie and Susan.

'You did it, George! I'm so proud!' said Eric, trying to hug George around the huge cardboard box.

'George! You were great,' said Annie rather shyly. 'I never thought you would be so good on stage. And your science was pretty amazing too.'

'Did I get it all right?' George asked her, feeling worried as Eric took the large box off him. 'I mean, when I said "billions", should I have said "tens of millions"? And when I talked about Jupiter, I thought maybe I should have said—'

'No!' said Annie. 'You got everything right, didn't he, Dad?'

Eric nodded and beamed at George. 'Especially the last bit. You got that really, really right. And you won first prize as well. You must be very happy.'

'I am,' said George, 'but there's just one problem. What are my parents going to say when I come home with a computer? They're going to be *so* angry.'

'Or they might be *so* proud,' said a voice.

George looked round and saw his dad, standing next to Susan. His jaw dropped. 'Dad?' he said. 'Were you here? Did you hear my speech about science?'

'I did,' said his dad. 'Your mother wanted me to come and collect you from school – she was worried about you this morning – and I got here in time to hear your talk. I'm very glad I did, George. Because you're right, we shouldn't be scared of science. We should use it to help us save the planet and not close our minds to it.'

'Does that mean I can keep my computer?' squeaked George.

George's dad smiled. 'Well, I think you deserve it. Only an hour a week, mind, or my home-made generator won't be able to keep up.'

There was a sudden commotion behind them and their little group was rudely pushed to one side by Dr Reeper, who was charging through the crowds in a great hurry. Following him were Ringo and the other members of his gang. They all looked in a furiously bad temper.

George watched them go and turned to Eric. 'Aren't you going to do something about Greeper? Like punish him?'

'Er, no,' said Eric sadly. 'I think Graham's punished himself quite enough already. Best leave him alone. I doubt our paths will cross again.'

'But . . . but . . .' said George. 'Eric, I wanted to ask you – how did Greeper know where to find you? I mean, you could have gone anywhere in the world, but he was waiting for you here and he was right. How did he know?'

'Ah well. The house next door to you,' said Eric. 'It belonged to my old tutor, the man in the photo with the beard.'

'But he disappeared!' said George.

'He only sort of disappeared,' replied Eric. 'I got a letter from him some time ago, saying he was going away on a very long journey and he didn't know if or when he'd be back. He told me he wanted me to have his house, in case I ever needed somewhere to work on Cosmos. He couldn't have imagined that Graham would lie in wait for me here, for all these years.'

'Where did the old man go?' asked George.

'He went . . .' Eric started.

'Home for tea,' said Susan very firmly. 'Can I give you a lift?' she asked George's dad.

'Oh no!' he said. 'I've got my bike. I'm sure we can balance the computer on the handlebars to get it home.'

'Dad!' huffed George. 'Please! We might drop it.'

'I don't mind running George home,' said Susan. 'It might be a bit of a squash but it's amazing what you can fit inside a Mini.'

Back at George's house that night, Eric, Susan and Annie all stayed for a delicious supper of home-grown vegetables eaten by candlelight at the kitchen table. Eric and George's dad got stuck into a long and very enjoyable argument about whether it was more important to look for a new planet or to try and save this one while Susan helped George to set up his shiny new computer.

Annie went out into the garden and fed Freddy, who was looking rather lonely in his sty. When she came back from chatting to the pig, she spent the evening dancing around George's mum, showing her all her ballet steps and telling her lots of tall stories which George's mum pretended to believe.

After they went home, leaving with lots of promises of eco-warriors talking to scientists at their conferences and trips to *The Nutcracker* together, George went upstairs to his room. He was very tired. He got into his pyjamas but he didn't close the curtains – he wanted to look out of the window as he lay under his duvet.

It was a clear evening and the night sky was studded with brilliant, twinkling stars. As he watched, a shooting star fell across the dark background, its long shiny tail blazing with light for a few seconds before it melted into nothing.

Perhaps the shooting star is a piece of the comet's tail, thought George to himself as he fell asleep. *As a comet passes the Sun, it warms up and the ice on it starts to melt . . .*

Acknowledgements

I am so grateful to the many people who kindly gave their support to the 'George' project. Tif Loehnis at Janklow and Nesbit has been wonderful throughout the whole process, as have all her staff at Janklow UK. Eric Simonoff at Janklow and Nesbit USA gave some truly stellar guidance. In Cambridge, Christophe Galfard made a huge contribution to the creative science storyline, imagery and detail. Judith Croasdell at DAMTP has been so patient, helpful and kind in getting us organized and providing invaluable advice. Joan Godwin deserves very special thanks for her tireless and generous back-up. Sam Blackburn for his technical support and work on the audio version. The amazing care team that surround my dad – for the dedication, affection and good humour that they bring to their work.

At Random House, I'd like to thank Philippa Dickinson, Larry Finlay and Annie Eaton for taking on the 'George' books with such enthusiasm and verve. And Shannon Park and Sue Cook for being so brilliant to work with on the project. Garry Parsons' charming illustrations have brought the story to life and I am totally indebted to James Fraser for designing such an eye-catching and beautiful front cover. Sophie Nelson and Julia Bruce for the very thorough copy-edit and proofread, Markus Poessel for his scientific fact-checking, Clare Hall-Craggs and Nina Douglas, Barry O'Donovan, Gavin Hilzbrich, Dan Edwards, Bronwen Bennie, Catherine Tomlinson, Juliette Clark and Maeve Banham for all their hard work, encouragement and good will.

As ever, enormous thanks to my mum and Jonathan, for everything they've done and for their unfailing kindness and endless support. But most of all, thanks to my cosmic dad. It's been such a great adventure. Thank you so much for giving me the chance to work with you. It's changed my Universe.

Lucy Hawking

LUCY HAWKING is the author of two novels
and has written for many British newspapers.
She lives in Cambridge with her son.

STEPHEN HAWKING is the Lucasian Professor of
Mathematics and Theoretical Physics at the University
of Cambridge. He is widely regarded as one of the
most brilliant theoretical physicists since Einstein.
His adult book *A Brief History of Time* was a huge
bestseller (over 12 million copies worldwide) and is
now available in more than 30 languages.

This is their first book together.

CHRISTOPHE GALFARD (PhD) is a former research student of Stephen Hawking and has collaborated on the scientific storyline, details and images within this book. Christophe now lives in France, where he works on explaining science in entertaining ways.

GARRY PARSONS is an award-winning illustrator of children's picture books and young fiction. In addition, his editorial and advertising illustrations appear regularly in Britain and the USA. Garry lives in London.

Join George in another dimension at
www.georgessecretkey.com

Explore even more of the Universe,
access exclusive content, enter
competitions, test your
knowledge and register
for free George updates!